RIDER

About the Author

Born in Derry, Northern Ireland, Peter was first published at the age of 17 in the Simon & Schuster anthology *Children of the Troubles*, edited by Laurel Holliday, and followed in quick succession by numerous other publications. His first novel was *The Camel Trail*.

Following a Bachelor's degree in Writing from London, Peter spent nineteen years in England where he worked his way from barman to advertising manager (and everything in between), before returning to his native Ireland in 2016.

Find Peter online at:
www.peterjmerrigan.co.uk

Twitter: @pjmerrigan140
Facebook: @authorpeterjmerrigan
Instagram: @pjmerrigan

Also by Peter J Merrigan

The Camel Trail
Lynch

RIDER
BOOK ONE

Peter J Merrigan

Managed by Nightsgale Books

Copyright © Peter J Merrigan, 2017

3 5 7 9 10 8 6 4 2

The right of Peter J Merrigan to be identified as the author of this Work has been asserted by him in accordance with the Copyright, Designs & Patents Act 1988

All rights reserved

First published 2012

This edition 2017 under management by
Nightsgale Books, Lifford, Ireland

www.nighstgale.com

ISBN 978 154816522 2

This publication may not be used, reproduced, stored or transmitted in any way, in whole or in part, without the express written permission of the author. Nor may it be otherwise circulated in any form of binding or cover other than that in which it has been published and without a similar condition imposed on subsequent users or purchasers.

All characters in this publication are fictitious and any similarity to real persons, alive or dead, is coincidental.

A CIP catalogue record of this book
is available from the British Library

For Mary, who told me
where I was going wrong.

And for Sue, who told me
where I was going right.

PART ONE

BELFAST

One

When Ryan's hand slipped out of Kane's and he fell with a suffocated gasp at his feet, Kane stood like an Edvard Munch painting, staring, as thick, dark blood seeped around his shoes. Ryan brought Kane to his knees as his bloodied hand wrestled with his leg, crimson liquid everywhere, Ryan's chest a weeping sore, a mouth gaping to the world. His dilated eyes fixed on Kane's and a question formed on his blood-stained lips: what had happened?

The squeal of car tires burned on the cold ground and an engine choked in the distance. And then Ryan's ragged breathing—like an old man on a respirator—consumed him.

He gargled, blood oozing from his mouth to stain his chin and neck, his eyes wide in horror and pain.

His dark lashes flickered over his green eyes as he stared up at Kane, his lips parting and a coughed sorry escaping before, with a quick and rasping breath, his body limped against the stone paving, one arm draped out over the kerb, fingers curled, uncurled.

Kane's knuckles were white as he gripped Ryan's hand and pulled it to his face, fresh blood smearing his cheek like war paint. He wanted to say something, but when he opened his mouth he had nothing to say. He choked on a sob as Ryan's vacant and lifeless eyes rolled up in their sockets to stare, unseeing, at the new moon. There was blood in his mouth as he clenched his lip between his teeth, tears blinding his eyes.

'Ryan?'

Kane pulled Ryan towards himself, his back rising from the ground, and he hugged him, rocking, embracing, crying. He was dimly aware of their surroundings, the club's doorway swinging open, the people crowding round, the screams — his screams? — that punctured the night.

His chest constricted, a cold fist crushing his lungs. 'It's okay, Ryan,' he whispered, his wet lips caressing Ryan's hand. 'It's okay. I'm here. It's all okay.'

And as he began losing his mind and his soul, as he began believing it was all okay, a hand touched his shoulder like the hand of God, a shivering tingle coagulating under his skin, and a distant voice pursed a desolate question. 'Are you all right?'

'It's okay. We're okay. It's okay,' he kept repeating.

'Are you hurt, honey?' the voice persisted.

He licked his lips with a parched tongue, tasting sweet warm blood, and looked up at the painted face of a drag queen covered in glitter like stars.

'Are you okay? Oh, God…Somebody call an ambulance.'

'I…' he began, but he said no more. He just looked at that face, his lips trembling, shoulders hunched to support the weight of Ryan Cassidy against the burden of his own pain. He closed his eyes and could feel the hot tears on his cheeks. 'I think he's dead,' he said; a revelation. 'I think he's dead.'

'Now listen, Kane…Kane?' The stocky paramedic nudged him and smiled. Kane blinked and looked at him. 'We're just going to run you over to the hospital; get you checked out, okay? You're suffering from shock. Do you under-stand?'

Kane looked at the mole on the paramedic's cheek that was edging through his stubble, his lips numb. What was he talking about?

'Are you on any medication? Have you taken anything?' He paused. He took Kane's elbow in his hand. 'Come on, let's get you into the ambulance and some place quiet, okay?'

Kane nodded stiffly and looked around. A couple of paramedics folded Ryan into a black rubber body bag and zipped it like a winking eye. There was blood on the ground. There were people on the other side of the police tape. There was a blinding camera flash. 'What happened?' someone asked. 'Keep rolling,' someone said.

The paramedics lifted Ryan on a stretcher. 'Where are they taking him?' Kane asked, confused.

'Mind your head as you step up. Careful,' said the man as he ushered him up into the back of the ambulance.

He sat, sighed, shivered. And he felt the ambulance pull away from the kerb. There was no siren. There was no emergency. His heart was already dead. And Ryan was no longer here.

—

He barely heard the police officer's questions as he stared across the hospital room at the window in the middle of the lilac wall. Outside, in the darkness, a light rain had begun to fall, stream-like gullies glistening down the pane like tears. His eyelids drooped to the heavy time of a ticking clock somewhere behind his head and he wondered what it was they had given him. A relaxant, they had called it. Something to take away the pain.

The officer asked his question for the third time.

With a polystyrene cup of lukewarm coffee nestled in his hands, Kane twisted his head from one side to the other, his neck stiff, shoulders knotted. Eight years. That's how long they had been together. Eight short years and nothing to show for it but a garbled spatter of memories in a shoebox, a patchwork of disembodied images and emotions.

'I think it'd be best if this was conducted in the morning,' a nurse said from behind him. 'Why don't you come back tomorrow.' It wasn't a question.

'Just one more thing,' the officer said. 'Mr Rider, did Ryan—?'

'Tomorrow,' her voice insisted.

The policeman snapped his notebook shut, his heavy shoes clanking over the polished floor as he left. 'I'll be right outside.'

The nurse came and stood in front of Kane. 'You must be exhausted,' she said, her voice soft, tender. She tried to take his bloodied shirt off but he wouldn't let her, pushing her away with his hands. 'Okay,' she said and she let him keep it on.

She pulled back the thick woollen blanket and helped him sit back. 'Is there anyone you'd like us to call? Friends? A family member?'

He looked up at her face. She was no older than

him.

Her face softened. 'Okay, we'll talk in the morning. Why don't you get some sleep, okay? The doctor gave you something to make it easier.' She patted the blanket where his leg was and absently checked the watch that hung from her breast pocket.

Kane let his head fall back to the pillows and looked up at her again. He could feel the effects of the sleepers they had given him. Almost inaudibly, he said, 'He's dead. Isn't he?'

'The doctor—'

'Isn't he?'

She bit her upper lip for a second, her hands smoothing some unseen wrinkles from her uniform. 'Yes.' She half looked away, as though it was painful even for her. 'Are you sure I can't call...?' Her voice trailed off, another sentence unfinished, another thought unsaid.

She smiled. He blinked. She turned and left the room. For a moment Kane was numb. And then, as his eyelids drooped involuntarily, his head lolling to one side in a diazepam-induced laziness, he felt a certain calm wash over him.

With the door closed and the florescent bulb overhead switched off, the only light came from the window across the room, a soft blue-white glow cast across the floor with shadows of rain-snakes twisting through it. He turned his head on the pillow and stared at the night beyond, a cold shiver nudging up his body. A tear dripped over the bridge of his nose. Somewhere below, in the morgue, Ryan Cassidy's pale and lifeless body was awaiting the coroner's inquest.

—

Hazed in a sleepy confusion, he awoke from a dream of Ryan, his laughter on his skin, his sweet, warm kisses and peanut butter breath. But reality was quick to expose the truth. A fortiori.

He sat up, the hospital bed firm underneath him, the pillows thick and concrete at his back. He sighed. He didn't think he could cry right then. Beyond the door of the room, he could hear a frantic voice paging an emergency. Room 6F. It wasn't him.

After taking in his surroundings, his eyes

adjusting to the dark, he slipped out of bed, pulled on his jeans and padded to the door. Outside, the police officer was asleep in a chair, stationed by his room as though he was a criminal. He stepped around him. The corridor was empty. He could hear the buzz of a vending machine and started towards it.

'Looking for the toilet?' a voice asked. Kane turned. Sitting at the nurses' station, an open magazine in front of her, a smile on her face, he recognised the nurse from earlier. He just blinked at her. 'It's down the hall,' she said, pointing.

'No,' he whispered, his voice a croak. 'I, ah, I just remembered…'

'What's that?' She leaned on the counter and her unbearable smile widened.

'There…there's going to be the funeral. I have to get things sorted.'

'Don't you worry about that tonight,' she said. From her accent, he thought she was from across the border. 'We can recommend some things for you in the morning. Why don't you get some sleep? I mean—'

'Can't,' he managed. 'Can't sleep.' He looked

away from her. The vending machine served tea and coffee of varying strengths and tastes. He looked back at the nurse. She looked at him.

Her smile faded. 'I know,' she said. 'I know.' Then she indicated the policeman outside Kane's room, her head nodding discreetly towards him. 'They're going to want to ask you some more questions in the morning. But if you're not up to it...'

He nodded absently, rummaging in his pocket and producing a ten pound note. 'You got change? For the machine?'

'It takes notes. Only got the thing installed two months ago.'

He pushed the money into the slot. 'You want one?' And he punched a button.

'No thanks,' the nurse laughed. 'I'm detoxing. It won't help you sleep, you know.'

When the vending machine spat the cup into the tray and the claw pulled back, he slid the glass cover aside and picked it up, a tiny spill of hot coffee burning his fingers. He turned back to the nurse and looked at her. And suddenly his lips trembled, his eyes full of tears and coffee-steam.

The coffee cup fell from his hand, splashing across the worn-tiled floor, and he sank down the wall, hunkering and hugging himself. 'Oh, God…' he breathed. 'Oh, God, Ryan…'

—

Kane looked up. The police car had stopped and the officer had cut the engine. The austere block of flats leered at him. He pressed his forehead against the window, the sun warming his face.

'This is it, right?' the officer asked.

Kane looked at him for a second, his lips burning and hacked, his mind clotted with a thick emptiness. 'You'll let me know?' he asked.

'As soon as we have any information. Detective Thorpe will probably drop by later, when he needs you.'

Kane nodded, looking up at the flats, too afraid to get out of the car.

When he reached for the door handle to let himself out, the officer cleared his throat. 'Look, if you need to speak to someone, a counsellor or something, you know?' He was trying to hand

Kane a bereavement information card.

Kane opened the door without accepting it and walked towards the whitewashed building. He didn't look back, but he knew the officer didn't drive away until he had reached the steps.

He went straight to his second-floor flat and locked the door behind him, and his eyes fell on the large painted canvas of Bette Davis on the wall. He had bought it as a present for Ryan. A lifetime ago.

—

It took half the afternoon before he was physically able to call Ryan's mother and her husband. He reached for the phone so many times, unable to pick it up. What would he say? How could he say it? When he finally found the courage and dialled, he got a message from their machine. We're off on business. David's got his mobile if it ever decides to work. Or call Kathy if it's important; she'll pass a message on. Adios.

He didn't have David's personal mobile number, but the phone book in the bedroom had his secretary's number, written in Ryan's careful script.

'Hi, Kane,' she beamed when he had identified himself. They had met once or twice but he'd always found her a little false, her personality straight out of the same bottle as her hair. 'They're off in Spain, lucky them. Is there something you need?'

'I, ah,' he stammered. 'Can you maybe give me their number over there?'

'Yeah, is everything all right? Where's the love of my life today?'

'Please, Kathy. There's been an accident.'

'Oh, God, is everything all right?'

'The number?'

'Of course,' she said. 'I understand.' She gave him the number, wished him well, and he put the receiver down.

He took a deep breath before dialling their hotel.

'*Hola. Hotel Melia Sancti Petri,*' the concierge said.

'*Señora Bernhard, por favor,*' he attempted in his limited Spanish.

'*Señora Bernhard?*'

'Yes. *Si*. It's very important.'

'One moment, please, sir.'

He heard the click of the phone as he was transferred. After two quiet rings, Margaret's voice filled his head. 'Hello?'

'Margaret,' he said. Tears were already clouding his vision.

Immediately, as though she already knew, her voice changed. 'Kane? Is something wrong? What's happened?'

He sighed. He sucked his lower lip into his mouth. There was music playing somewhere behind Margaret, a flirty Spanish number. He blinked away the tears, blinked again. A sob caught in his throat like an ulcer.

'Kane?' Margaret repeated. 'Where's Ryan?'

He broke down, a man beaten to a pulp. He could not say it; didn't need to.

The silence on the other end of the line was wholly tangible. It felt like the air had been sucked out of the room and he was in a vacuum, his chest tight, heart thumping.

'No. Please, no,' she whispered.

—

'We're appealing for anyone with information to come forward,' Detective Thorpe said as he sat across from Kane in the living room of his empty flat, Bette Davis shining down on them like the Divine Judge. 'But due to the suddenness of the attack, no one saw the guy's face. CCTV didn't even catch it.'

'So he gets off scot-free?' Kane asked. He could see clearly, every time he closed his eyes, the knife wound on Ryan's chest.

'We're doing all we can to find out who it was. Is there anyone Mr Cassidy might not have seen eye-to-eye with?'

'No,' Kane said. 'No, everyone loved him.'

He wove his fingers together in his lap and looked at the man. Thorpe was unshaven and his shirt was wrinkled, a thick shag of ginger hair falling down over his forehead.

Thorpe eyed the Bette Davis picture on the wall and looked back at Kane. 'Work colleagues?' he suggested. 'Maybe a friend he fell out with?'

Kane shook his head. 'He was everyone's best

friend.' When he noticed Thorpe's unease, the glances at the canvas, he said, 'Bette Davis. She was an actress.'

Thorpe nodded. 'Not quite Audrey Hepburn, is she?' He smiled and stood. 'Well,' he said, 'if you think of anything that might help us, let me know. The coroner's interim report is due in later today. Are you going to be all right?'

Kane closed his eyes. 'I'll be fine,' he said and he showed him to the door.

He went to the kitchen, poured a coffee and watched it go cold. Sitting there, staring vacantly at the microwave, the room grew dark and close around him.

Finally, pulling out of his reverie, he locked the door and checked the windows, then draped his jeans over the back of a chair and went to bed, blinking in the dark, tired but unable to sleep, his mind thick with fragments of useless memories, useless thoughts.

If they had stayed for one more drink, one more dance…

He closed his eyes, listened to his breathing, short and heavy, and bit his lip.

It was only in the morning, as the phone invaded his broken dreams, that he realised he must have fallen asleep. He awoke from the foetal position he had curled into around a pillow and stared dumbly at the phone for a minute before awkwardly grasping the receiver.

'Hello?'

'Mr Rider. This is Detective Thorpe. We spoke yesterday? The interim report is in on your friend, Mr Cassidy. I think you should come down to the station if you don't mind.'

'The station?' Kane asked, still groggy from sleep.

Detective Thorpe paused for the slightest hesitation. 'There are a few things we'd like to discuss.'

Two

Detective James Thorpe showed Kane into his office at the police station on Antrim Road and he took a seat. When Thorpe sat down opposite him, behind his messy desk, he smiled.

Kane looked at him. 'You said there was a problem?'

'I said there are a few things we'd like to discuss.'

'Is something wrong?'

'In a manner of speaking,' he said.

'What is it?'

He drank from a disgusting-looking mug of tea. 'I'm sorry, would you like a drink? The tea's like tar and the water cooler is warm, but you're welcome to it.'

'Can you tell me what's going on?' Kane

pressed.

'Mr Rider—Kane—how well did you know the deceased?'

'Eight years. Why?'

'And you've been...partners—is that right?—for eight years also.'

'Yes.'

'You had a good relationship?'

'I loved him.'

'Yes, and you shared a flat?' He consulted a sheet of paper from a file on his desk. 'Six years, you told my colleagues.'

'Yeah, about six years.' Kane looked at the paper but couldn't make out what it said, then looked back at Thorpe. 'What's going on?'

'Mr Rider,' Thorpe said. 'There's no easy way to say this. Some routine blood-work on the deceased, Ryan Cassidy, showed up a few anomalies.'

'What sort of anomalies?'

'Were you aware of Mr Cassidy's addiction to heroin?'

He couldn't think. His head felt light and his fingers went numb.

When Thorpe spoke again, his voice was only a vague whisper in Kane's ear. 'We need a blood sample from you. It's in your best interest to submit one voluntarily.'

—

Kane scratched uselessly at the corner of the plaster on his arm, the mark of Thorpe's blood-sample request, and stared at the blank TV screen. The remote control was in his hand but he hadn't turned it on.

Heroin. How had he missed it? Why didn't he see the signs? But then, he had to admit he didn't know what the signs were. Had Ryan's mood ever changed? Were those big wide eyes natural or induced?

Thorpe had told him where Ryan had injected himself. There weren't many needle-marks, but enough that he should have spotted them if he'd been looking properly.

His mind was listless, wandering from one splinter of thought to another. He thought back to two nights ago. He and Ryan had just come out of the nightclub. Ryan had been trying to talk him into going to a party at someone's house. He forgot who.

Ryan had taken his hand and they walked along the street towards the nearest taxi rank. That was when a man bumped into him. The guy could have been their age, could have even been a teenager or someone in his forties; his hoodie hid his face.

It was a split-second affair. 'Sorry, mate,' the guy had said. And he kept walking. And then Ryan was on the ground, a gaping knife wound in his chest and fear in his eyes. Kane had given no more thought to that man until much later when he told Thorpe.

The phone rang and pulled him from sinister thoughts. He scratched the edge of the plaster again and rose to pick up the receiver. 'Hello?'

But there was no one there.

—

Two years ago, he had sat between Ryan's legs facing out onto the Atlantic from a quiet corner of Portstewart where they often spent the weekends in the summer months. Ryan's chin was resting on Kane's neck, his arms around his shoulders, his breath warm and sensual on his cheek. Their skin was still wet from a recent swim, where he had caught Kane in the water, held him tight, and kissed him. The sun was going down, melting into the ocean, its liquid-gold rays reaching out to them like the spreading fingers of Neptune, shimmering, inviting.

Ryan had kissed his neck. 'Don't you wish it could be like this forever? Just us, with the world at our feet?'

'Why can't it?' Kane asked, stifling a sleepy yawn. He collected some sand in his hand and let it trickle through his fingers.

'Because things happen,' Ryan said wistfully. He hugged Kane tighter. 'Because people are always changing. Because nothing ever stays the same.'

'The song remains the same,' Kane joked.

Ryan's fingers trailed along Kane's collarbone. 'No matter how hard you try, it's all going to be different. You can't keep a bird in a cage and expect it to sing like it did when it was free. The world is a nightmare place and we're all too fucked up to care.'

'Stop going all Baby Jane on me,' Kane said, collecting more sand.

'But don't you feel sometimes that things would be better if nothing ever changed? Because once it changes, you'll never get it back. Once it's gone...' His voice drifted away, his grip around Kane's body loosening.

'That's a bit deep,' Kane laughed, his back pressing against Ryan's chest.

'I'm serious,' Ryan said. When Kane dusted his hands off and turned to face him, he noticed the tears in his eyes. 'Would you still love me if something changed you? Or me?'

—

Against his boss' express wishes, Kane went back to work at Kestrel Solutions that afternoon. He had taken on a three-week temp contract in telesales with them over two years ago but loved the job so much they let him stay. He could sell redemption to the devil, Ryan had told him and he was doubling his earnings on commission from that first week. They were a telecoms solutions company that prided themselves on UK call centres and both their incoming and outgoing sales calls were routed through local centres. Kane's base in Belfast served the whole of Northern Ireland.

After fixing himself a coffee from the breakout area, he returned to his station and placed his next call, a follow-up on a recent sales prospect in Limavady. Behind him, at the water cooler, a couple of his colleagues stared at him behind his back. They had all heard the news about his boyfriend's death—murder, they were calling it— and no one had expected him back so soon. But the office gossip would slither around him and nobody would dare mention it to him beyond asking him how he was.

'Mr Campbell, please,' Kane said into his headset when he spoke to a receptionist. 'This is Kane Rider from Kestrel Solutions.'

He waited to be put through and stared at his computer screen. If he looked at any of his colleagues he would see the pity in their eyes and it would break him.

'John?' Kane said when Mr Campbell came on the line. 'Kane Rider. How've you been? Have you had a chance to go over the quote I provided last week?'

He could feel their eyes boring into his back.

'I have,' John Campbell said. 'And I just have a few questions, if that's okay?'

'Fire away,' Kane said, positioning his fingers on his keyboard to take notes.

He could hear their whispered words all around him.

'You said it was the latest model?'

'Absolutely,' Kane said. 'I can guarantee it's fresh off production and if you take the six-year warranty you won't have any problems.'

He could sense their desperate need to find out the truth.

'The twenty-five per cent discount is a special limited-time offer, John. I'd hate for you to miss out.'

'Can you leave it with me for another twenty-four hours?' John asked.

Kane said, 'Let me just see if I can hold the discount open for you, John. I'll be two seconds.'

He put the call on hold, removed his headset and buried his face in his hands.

Breaking through the force field he had erected around himself, his boss came up and sat on the edge of his desk. Jill Ruthers was middle-aged but could still pass for twenty-something.

'Kane,' she said.

He kept his face in his hands, his elbows on the desk.

'I just…We all wanted to say…'

He looked up at her, nodded, begged her with his eyes not to finish her sentence.

She saw his desk phone was on hold and said, 'Finish the call and go home. I'll pay you for the rest of the week. Call me on Friday afternoon and we'll talk about next week, see if you need any extra time off.'

Jill had met Ryan on several occasions when he had stopped by after work to catch a ride home with Kane. They had got talking one day as they waited for Kane to finish a call and had managed to arrange a night out, but it had never happened.

Kane closed his eyes and Jill touched his shoulder. 'Go home,' she repeated.

He watched her as she walked away, called after her. When she turned back to him, he said, 'Thanks.' He put his headset back on and took the call off hold. 'John, mate, good news. I've spoken to my manager and she's agreed to extend the discount until tomorrow. Can we give you a call around noon?'

As he hung up, his mobile phone buzzed silently in his pocket. He took it out and answered it.

But the line went dead.

—

To take his mind off everything, Kane went to the gym. Margaret was due back from Spain in the early hours of tomorrow morning; it was the first available flight she could get. He didn't know how he could face her. Ryan was her only child and they had relied on each other through Ryan's father's descent into and eventual consumption by dementia praecox and a brain tumour that swiftly killed him in his early forties. They had nursed each other through the ensuing heartache while

Ryan was nothing more than a child but suddenly the man of the house. When Margaret's new husband came along, it was a welcome relief for all.

Only a couple of people worked the machines — a woman on a rowing machine, her short ponytail swinging behind her head, and a man, muscles straining beneath sweaty skin, puffing air in time as he bench-pressed.

Kane started up on a treadmill at the other side of the gym, his earphones in, iPod strapped to his arm, his feet slapping out a rhythm to match the music. He stared blank ahead, could feel sweat trickling down his back. It was total focus. When he ran, he felt nothing. His legs did all the hard work.

He wiped beads of perspiration from his forehead, running like he was going somewhere, running like he was leaving somewhere.

On the floor beside the treadmill, sitting on top of his sports bag and almost lost in the folds of a towel, his phone lit up from an incoming call. It caught his eye and he glanced at it, but he didn't feel like talking to anyone. He looked straight ahead again, his feet punishing the treadmill, and he cranked up the speed on the display.

The phone kept flashing, ringing.

Kane kept running.

And the phone stopped, its screen dimming, a small light flashing to tell him he'd missed a call.

He ran faster. Going nowhere. Going anywhere.

When the phone started ringing again, he shook his head. He didn't want to stop, but he did. He slowed the pace, looked at the phone, hopped off the treadmill and pulled his earphones out.

He picked up the phone and the towel, wiping sweat from his face before answering it. 'Hello?'

He raised a leg, folded the knee—it felt stiff—and someone skinned past him, knocking him off balance. He dropped his foot to the floor for support and the phone slipped from his hand. The man, in a hoodie and baggy black jeans, pushed his way into the male changing rooms at the far end.

It was him. He knew it was. The man who killed his boyfriend was in his gym.

Momentary shock gave way and Kane ploughed across the gym after him. When he burst into the changing rooms, a man with a towel round his waist was about to remove it but he stopped. He stared at Kane but Kane ignored him. He looked along each bench, down each row of lockers, in the shower stalls. But no one was there.

'Did you see a man?' Kane asked the towel guy.

'What man?'

He shook his head. Daunted, he returned to the gym room and picked up his phone where it had fallen. The call was still active.

Bringing it back to his ear, Kane said, 'Who is this?'

The woman was no longer rowing. She was standing next to the machine and stretching her limbs.

'What the hell do you want?' he said into the phone.

The woman stopped stretching, one hand on an elbow, arm across her body. 'Excuse me?'

Kane hit end on the phone. 'Sorry,' he said. He picked up his bag and headed back to the changing room. He was losing the thread.

—

The late summer sun leached across the darkening sky as he pulled up outside his block of flats.

The song never remains the same.

He got out, grabbed his sports bag, locked the car and turned, glimpsing a light in the window of his flat. A shadow passed across it and the light went out.

It was almost as if he hadn't seen it. After two steps forward, he had to stop and think. He was tired. He wasn't thinking straight. It was the neighbour's place. It had to be.

But what if it wasn't?

He headed towards the entrance, his heart rate elevated, pulling out his keys and fingering for the right one without even looking down at them. As he approached, the door swung open and two men came out, hoods up, heads down. They quickly disappeared into the night.

He stood there, catching his breath, feeling a sharp pain at the bottom of his sternum from the fear. Inside, the buttons for the lift showed it was on the sixth floor. He took the stairs.

Kane's front door was still locked, no sign of forced entry. Along the corridor, a neighbour's voice raised and was echoed by his wife. Something smashed.

It was someone else's light he had seen. Or maybe no light at all.

He opened the door, pushed it wide. He didn't step in until he felt sure there was no one inside. He switched on all the lights and opened every door. He even looked under the bed like a frightened child.

Nothing.

It was only when he returned to the living room to look out of the window that he noticed the small white envelope on the coffee table. Kane Rider was printed in bold lettering across the front of it. His heart thumped in his chest. He didn't know whether to open it, call the cops, or just get the hell out of there.

He thought about doing all three.

As he reached across for the envelope, he glanced around the room. Was he really alone? He tore the envelope open with shaking hands.

Inside, there was a piece of white cardboard the size of a business card. He pulled it out. Nothing else.

And scrawled across one side were the words:

*Vengeance is mine, and recompense,
for the time when their foot shall slip;
for the day of their calamity is at hand,
and their doom comes swiftly.*

Three

Kane looked across at Thorpe as he talked to a forensic technician who was dusting the door for fingerprints. A couple of uniformed police officers milled around, looking, for all their sense of importance, as useless as Kane felt.

'You'll be getting your locks changed, of course,' Thorpe said when he approached him. 'And I'll station a man outside for the rest of the night.' He held up the small card in an evidence bag. 'I'll have this looked at, but if our man is clever enough to get into your flat unseen, my guess is we're not going to find anything.'

'So that's it?' Kane asked, incredulous.

Thorpe shrugged. 'Like I said, we'll take a closer look at this. Do you want a car placed outside?'

'Do you think I need one?'

Thorpe knit his ginger eyebrows together.

'Look, I know what you're thinking. It's probably not connected. All we can—'

Kane interrupted him. 'You seriously think this isn't connected? "Vengeance is mine"?'

'We're looking at the options, that's all,' he said. 'Ninety-nine times out of a hundred, violent crime ends there.'

'What about the other one time?' Kane asked.

'I'm not going to lie to you, Kane. We don't know what we're dealing with yet. But without any hard evidence, a fingerprint, a hair—anything—there isn't a lot we can do tonight. I'm really sorry for your loss, but until we turn something up, there's little to be done. Just sit tight until we know more.'

Kane turned away from him but quickly turned back, looking him directly in the eyes. 'The other one time out of a hundred: does that end with the boyfriend getting killed, too?'

—

To wake at four in the morning and smile, to have the feeling that your loved one lies beside you, in sleep, and then to shudder in a rush of reality — the feeling is agonizing. He turned on his pillow, away from the place Ryan should have been lying.

He was dead.

Kane had to keep repeating it in his head, unbelieving, questioning. And then the thought of the sinister calling card, the thought that someone had gotten into his flat, his home, the thought that perhaps his own life was at risk. And why?

He could not know.

In the parking lot below, a police car loitered. A visible deterrent. The officer inside, Kane could imagine, would be drinking lukewarm coffee. Maybe he had one leg out of the open door. Maybe he was radioing the dispatch girl. Maybe he was reading a Tom Clancy.

Maybe he was asleep.

He went to the window. The car wasn't there.

Panic set in like a heart attack. He wanted to go to the phone, wanted to stay at the window. His reflection in the glass stared back at him. Had something happened? Was the officer called away on an emergency?

And then the car came back around the corner

and pulled to a stop outside the building opposite. He'd obviously been doing a tour of the block.

Kane sighed. He actually laughed.

And then his mobile vibrated on the bedside cabinet.

It only occurred to him as he lifted the phone to wonder who would be calling in the middle of the night.

He was greeted with silence. Again.

'Who is this?'

He thought he heard something in the background, but it could have been the blood pounding in his ears. He looked towards the window. Could he attract the officer's attention from up here?

'Hello?' he said again.

He was about to end the call when someone spoke. 'Mr Rider. I do hope I didn't wake you.'

'Who is this?' he repeated.

'I see you have some company outside. Nice to see you're not lonely. Do you read the Bible, Mr Rider?'

'What do you want?'

His throat was tight.

'I'm an acquaintance of someone you know. Oh, I'm sorry. Someone you knew.'

'What?'

'Please, Mr Rider, you know who I mean. Did you get my note?'

'What note?' Kane went back to the window and stared down at the stationary police car below. 'What do you want from me?' he asked.

'Your friend owes me something. I'll be in touch. And don't bother telling your nice police friends. I'm sure you realise what I can do to you. Goodbye.'

—

He was pacing and he couldn't stop it. His head hurt, his ribs felt like they were contracting around his lungs. With every step towards the window, he tugged at the curtain. The police car was still there. The driver sat in darkness.

He had the distinct feeling that he was being watched, that no matter what he did, where he went, he would be seen. If he went downstairs and told the cop, they'd know. If he phoned Thorpe, they'd know. Was his phone tapped? Could they do that?

They say a madman doesn't know he's mad. Kane began to wonder if there were microphones hidden behind books, if there were tiny surveillance cameras in tiny discreet corners. Was Jimmy Stewart watching him through a zoom lens from a window across the way?

None of it was making sense. Ryan had been stabbed. Someone had been in Kane's flat. Someone had just threatened him. And for all he knew, there was absolutely no reason why.

Your friend owes me something.

He glanced out the window again.

I'll be in touch.

And then someone knocked on his front door. He hesitated, looked at the phone that was still in his hand, and cautiously entered the living room.

When the knock rasped again, he called out, 'Who is it?'

'It's the police, Mr Rider. Officer Richards.'

He unlocked and opened the door, leaving the security chain on so that the door could only open a couple of inches. When Officer Richards flashed his badge and his best smile, Kane let him in.

'I saw your light was on,' he said. 'Is everything okay?'

'Uh, yeah,' Kane said. 'I mean...' He didn't know what to say to him.

'It's stifling outside. I don't know how anyone can sleep in this heat. Do you mind if I use your toilet?'

Kane eyed him suspiciously and Richards smiled again.

'Toilet?' Kane asked. 'Yeah, sorry, it's that way.'

Richards could tell he was agitated. 'Are you okay?'

'I'm fine,' he said. 'It's just...been a long night. Can't sleep.'

'Too hot,' Richards said.

'Yeah.'

He nodded sympathetically and headed towards the bathroom. He left the door open and Kane could hear him urinating.

'Look,' Kane said, 'I'm not going to sleep any more tonight. Do you want a coffee or something?'

From the bathroom, Richards said, 'I should probably get back to the car.' The toilet flushed. He came back out, zipping up his trousers as he did so. 'But why not?'

—

Officer Richards stood by the window, inattentively scuffing the toe of his shoe in the carpet. Kane offered him another coffee, noting the tiredness on his face. He yawned, accepted, and toyed with the curtain.

Kane stood next to him, his hands cupping his elbows, coffee cooling on the windowsill, and stared out into the ocean of buildings and late-for-work faces below like rats racing.

Richards blew on his coffee before sipping from the mug, thin tendrils of steam pushing out towards the window. 'You want a lift to the hospital this morning?'

Kane sucked on his upper lip and shook his head. Instead, he said, 'How long have you been — ?'

'Sitting outside people's houses?' Richards said, smiling.

'A police officer.'

'Twelve years. Used to be a milkman, but all those early starts, you know?'

'So now you sit outside people's houses all night.'

'Yeah.'

It was small talk. Kane had nothing to say to him—nothing he dared to say. Even though he wanted him to stay, he also wanted him to leave.

When the phone rang, Kane's pulse quickened, his eyes darting between the phone and Richards.

'You want me to get that?' Richards asked.

Kane just looked at him. After another ring, the officer moved and picked up the receiver. Kane held his breath.

'Hello?' Richards said.

There was a pain in Kane's chest.

'No, I'm not Mr Rider. Who's calling?'

Kane clenched his jaw.

'I'll just put him on,' Richards said. He held the receiver to his chest. 'Margaret,' he whispered.

Kane breathed again and took the phone. The officer stepped back to the window and his coffee. Margaret was back in Belfast and ready to meet Kane at the hospital. David, she said, was still in

Spain. She had insisted he stay there to close whatever important deal it was he needed to close.

When he sat the phone back down, the officer looked at him questioningly. 'Ryan's mother,' Kane told him. 'She's meeting me at the hospital.'

Richards nodded and finished his coffee. 'Thanks,' he said. 'Shall I show myself out? I'm sure you have things to do.'

He hesitated. Perhaps Kane's face revealed his fear.

'You have Detective Thorpe's direct number, right? Just give him a call if you need him. For anything.'

He shook Kane's hand and turned to leave.

'Officer?'

He stopped. 'Yeah?'

'I...Well, thanks.'

He was going to tell him about the call, but he could hear that voice threatening him. Would he know? Kane's eyes were pleading with Officer Richards but he couldn't verbalise his pain.

'No problem,' Richards said. 'Goodbye.'

Kane locked the door behind him and went back to the window. He watched as Richards exited the building and walked to his car, got in and drove away. With his breath fogging the windowpane, he stared at the police car is it turned a corner and disappeared.

Your friend owes me something. I'll be in touch.

Four

The hospital morgue was cold, the walls sweating damp. Kane closed his eyes. Ryan looked like a teenager, like a sick kid, his skin a dappled grey, his cheeks slightly sunken. Kane looked away and ran a hand over his face.

'I'll wait outside,' the doctor said.

Kane sat in the chair and clasped his fingers together, inhaling deeply and breathed out through puffed-up cheeks. He looked at Ryan. He seemed restful and at peace.

Kane bit his lip.

The wound on Ryan's chest, under the sheet, had been sewn up, Kane was told. He wanted to see it but his hand wouldn't pull the sheet back. His eyes filled with tears.

The door behind him opened. 'Kane?'

He turned, brushing at his tears with his sleeve.

'Oh, Kane, no...'

Margaret Bernhard rushed to him, falling into his arms as he stood. They sobbed together, their tears fusing on their cheeks, her arms about his shoulders. Then she turned away, steadying her breathing.

'I can't look,' she admitted.

Kane touched her shoulder.

'I can't believe it, Kane. Is this real?'

'I wish it wasn't.'

They were silent. Margaret took his hand and turned. Her lips trembled, eyes puffy and red. She stepped forward, bracing her strength against the chair.

She looked at Ryan.

'Oh, my baby,' she exhaled and she sobbed again, her hand on his face.

And right then, seeing the grief on Margaret's face, feeling the pain like Death himself had jabbed him with his scythe, Kane couldn't help thinking, Did Ryan bring this on himself? Was it his own fault that he lay now, as he did, naked in life's own mortality?

Kane put a hand to the pain at his breastbone. He could feel his heart beating.

'Baby,' Margaret said again. She kissed Ryan's forehead, both his cheeks, and finally his lips. And she took his hands and joined them together as if in prayer. She whispered something in his ear, a blessing maybe, and she turned away from him.

—

They sat together opposite Detective Thorpe in his office. 'I won't believe it,' Margaret had said. She was wringing a tissue in her hands while Kane sat passively beside her, staring at the floor.

Thorpe had invited them here to go over the case history with Margaret.

'I understand how you feel,' Thorpe said.

Margaret shook her head adamantly. 'No, it isn't possible. Not Ryan.' She turned to Kane. 'Tell him, Kane.'

'They have evidence,' Kane said, his voice weak. It felt like a betrayal.

'I don't care what they have,' she said. 'I know he wouldn't do drugs.'

Thorpe stood and cleared his throat. 'It's a lot to take in. I understand. Believe me I do. Mrs Bernhard, I—'

She shook her head again, looked at Kane. 'Do you believe him?'

'I...'

'You believe he was doing drugs?'

'No,' he said. 'I don't know.'

She took his hands in her own, held them tight. 'In all the time you've known him, have you ever seen him do drugs?'

'No. But...'

She let go of his hands, folded her arms. To Thorpe, she said, 'As soon as you find out who murdered my son, you'll call me. And you tell them—tell them I'll visit them in jail every day for the rest of my life so that they'll never forget the face of the mother they made childless. You tell them that.'

She stood up, faced Thorpe over the mountain of paperwork on his desk, and then she turned and left.

Kane caught up with her as she was heading towards the front door of the building and they exited together, walking down the steps and towards his car. Margaret's resolve was ebbing, her shoulders slumped, head lowered, her movements slow and deliberate.

Kane pulled his car keys out of his jacket pocket, triggered the central locking and opened the passenger door for her. She stopped, her hand on the edge of the door, and looked back at the police station. She looked at him, her face saddened, and then she eased herself into the car. He had never seen her look so old.

When he closed the door and walked around the front of the car, he noticed a slip of paper tucked under one of the windscreen wipers. He hesitated before picking it up and unfolding it, looking around as he did so.

It was a hand-scrawled note: I said no police.

There was nobody around, nobody that looked to be following him or watching him. He took a deep breath, scrunched the paper into a ball and stuffed it in his pocket.

In his car, when he got behind the wheel, Margaret said, 'What was that?' There was no real interest in her voice.

Kane started the ignition, checked his mirrors. 'Just one of those stupid flyers,' he lied. 'Ten per cent off something or other.' When he pulled away from the roadside, the skin on his hands stretched tight over his knuckles as he gripped the steering wheel. His chest was still aching.

—

A light rain spat at the funeral party as they gathered around a newly dug grave, indolently watching the young Father Mitchell as he led them in prayer. Margaret, in her black trouser suit, strengthened perhaps by the arrival of David late last night, sympathetically squeezed Kane's arm before she placed a white carnation on top of the coffin. White for purity, Kane thought.

'Eternal rest,' Father Mitchell prayed, 'grant unto Ryan, O Lord, and let perpetual light shine upon him.'

Reading from the Order of Service, the gathered people replied, 'May his soul, and the souls of all the faithful departed, rest in peace. Amen.'

Only a few of Ryan's friends turned out. Some of

them Kane recognised, but there were others, people he had never seen before. He wondered if they knew about Ryan's addiction, wondered if they were in on it, if they supplied him. More to the point, he wondered if any of them knew about the phone calls he had been receiving. Or the biblical calling card.

He loosened the tie around his neck, his face feeling flushed in the rain. When the funeral was over and people were leaving, they shook his hand or gave him a gentle hug, accompanied by words of condolences.

John, the only drag queen Kane and Ryan really knew, who called herself Daphne Do-More when it suited, was a completely different person today, the only time Kane had ever seen him in a suit and without the face paint. His stubble must have been a couple of days old. Everyone hides behind a mask. It was Wilde who'd said you only see someone's true self when you give them a mask.

Kane wasn't so sure.

Margaret resembled a pillar, brave-faced and strong. Kane imagined she was tearing herself up inside, but outwardly, she gave nothing away.

She approached him and pointed to a group of Ryan's friends who were clambering into a car. 'They're going to a pub. One that they say Ryan used to go to.'

He looked away from her. He was crying. David, grey-haired and upright, stepped away to give them a moment, his hands behind his back like an army general. Kane's words were gritty when he spoke. 'They're going to get drunk in his memory?'

Margaret touched his shoulder. 'They're going to toast him. He'd like that.'

'I think he'd prefer to be alive.'

'We'd all prefer it if he was alive.'

Kane turned away from her. He clenched his teeth and his eyes, his hands knuckling his temples. 'It's not f-fair,' he said, his voice pathetic, ripped through with sobs. Margaret Bernhard took him in her arms and said the truest thing he'd ever heard.

'Life isn't fair.'

—

He needed some time alone, some time to collect himself. He told Margaret he wouldn't be long, that he'd see them back at theirs within the hour. And now, sitting on the damp grass in another part of the cemetery, he stared at the headstone in front of him. In loving memory of Laura Rider, cherished mother. B. 6-9-1956 – D. 24-3-2008. Taken too soon.

Cancer had consumed her a few years ago and Ryan had been his rock. And now here he was, going through the motions all over again. Without Ryan, he wasn't sure he could manage it this time. Without Ryan, without the strength that he had given him, Kane wasn't sure he even wanted to manage this time.

In his trouser pocket, his phone vibrated and he closed his eyes. If heaven really existed, like his mother had believed, he hoped she was there to meet Ryan.

And yet — the drugs.

Part of him still couldn't believe it. If it was true — and it had to be — then he was more stupid than he could have imagined. You can't live with someone, sleep with someone, and not notice the puncture wounds on his arm — on his groin, for heaven's sake. Thorpe had told him that the coroner had found a couple of small needle-marks in the area between his leg and his testicles. Not an uncommon thing, Thorpe said, for users to hide their addiction among pubic hair.

The thought made him sick.

His phone continued to vibrate but he refused to answer it. He knew whose voice would be on the other end, knew beyond any doubt.

And he could go screw himself today.

—

Everyone had gathered at David and Margaret's house after the funeral. David, a financial magnate with a keen eye for a good deal, had been clever with his money; he had bought a plot of land on the northern outskirts of Belfast and employed a team of builders to construct not just a house, but a mansion. Hidden from the road by a line of trees and an electronic gate, he had been conscious of security and installed CCTV. In their teenage years, before moving in together, Kane and Ryan had spent many summer evenings by the covered pool under the watchful gaze of motion-sensor cameras.

It was there that they had their first kiss, there that they shared their first sexual experience, hurried and immediate as it was, lying naked beside each other under nothing but a blanket and the wan light of the moon. It was there that they had first said, 'I love you.'

The funeral had been wonderful, people said. Ryan would have loved it, they told him. Good old Irish logic. He stopped himself from stating the obvious.

Kane stood by the glass display cabinet of hunting trophies and photos of David and Margaret with their clay-pigeon friends. It was a sport that never appealed to Ryan or Kane.

His head was hurting. 'You should have another whiskey,' Daphne Do-More's alter ego, John, said. He had come back from the pub that the guys had gone off to in order to extend his condolences. He scratched the stubble at his neck and said, 'All I can think about doing is getting pissed.'

Kane smiled, obliging, and looked around. It was odd seeing John without the wig and make-up, odder still seeing him without Ryan around.

Margaret, from a place near the front door, caught Kane's eye and smiled at him. She and David were circling the room, Margaret with a platter of sandwiches cut into little triangles, David with a whiskey decanter.

Kane sighed, turned back to John, and said, 'Sorry, John, do you mind? I need a bit of air.'

He headed towards the front door, but Father Mitchell had just come in and he couldn't face another well-intended comment about Ryan. Instead, he ducked through into the kitchen and took the rear stairs up to the next floor.

There were six bedrooms but never more than three had ever been used at once. David and Margaret shared the westernmost room, the master bedroom, and Ryan's old room, still filled with his teenage life, was on the opposite side of the house. The rest were made up for guests and cleaned weekly.

Kane paused outside Ryan's old room, his fingers on the handle, and he pressed his forehead against the cold wood of the door. Then he entered.

It hadn't changed. Everything from the framed

film posters on the walls to the scattering of teenager's techno-toys that Ryan had seen fit to leave behind when he moved into the flat with Kane lay exactly as Kane had remembered them.

He ran his finger over the spines of the old horror novels on the bookcase that Ryan loved so much, soaked himself in the room's history, and sat on the edge of the king-size bed. From the moment David had married Margaret, they had lived in luxury. Neither boy had spoken much of their fathers. Kane's dad had done a runner when he was three, leaving his mum to raise Kane on her own, and Ryan's dad had died years before Kane met him.

On the cabinet beside the bed, standing up in an ornate silver frame, was a photo of Kane and Ryan on a skiing trip when they were seventeen, Ryan's arm over Kane's shoulder, their sun goggles on their foreheads and toothy smiles on their faces. Kane picked it up and wondered, momentarily, why Ryan had left it behind. But their flat was filled with photos of other happy occasions. Ryan was seldom without his camera. He had developed his passion for photography from Margaret and, ever indulgent of his wife's desires, David had built a darkroom for them behind the kitchen on the ground floor.

Kane remembered the first time he'd been in Ryan's bedroom, not long after they had first met. At sixteen, Ryan joined Kane's school in the last term before their GCSEs after David had moved them from South Belfast when the house building had been completed. They hit it off almost immediately.

One evening, after school, Ryan had brought Kane over while his parents were at an awards ceremony in town. Kane had been sitting here on the side of the bed, flipping through a stack of CDs, and said, 'You can't put Billie Holiday next to Urban Dance Classics.'

'You don't even know who Billie Holiday is,' Ryan objected.

It was true. But Kane held up the cover and said, 'Doesn't look like dance music to me.'

Ryan had grabbed the case, sat it on the bed, and picked up his iPod. 'You'll love her,' he said. 'I love all that old stuff. Music, films, books. I should have been born in the twenties.'

Kane had laughed. 'You'd be like a hundred years old!'

Ryan unravelled the earphones and passed one to Kane, who took it dubiously. He scanned for a track and said, 'Listen.'

Kane put the earphone in his ear and Ryan shifted closer, putting the spare earphone in his own ear. They sat side by side, their legs almost touching, as Ryan mouthed the words of You Don't Know What Love Is in time to Billie's melodic voice.

Kane couldn't concentrate on the song. All he could think of was Ryan's leg, just there, the creases of their school trousers almost caressing each other. He looked up at Ryan's face and Ryan looked back. They stared at each other.

And Ryan smiled. Electric.

Kane pulled back from the memory when Ryan's door opened and Margaret entered. 'Thought I'd find you up here,' she said.

He placed the photo back on the bedside cabinet and Margaret came and sat next to him on the bed.

She took his hand and leaned her head on his shoulder. They said nothing. In time, Kane put an arm around her and they stared at the framed photo together, each lost in thought, perhaps each of them battling with the demons of their past.

David popped the lids off two bottles of beer and sat them on the kitchen table, easing himself into a chair. He pushed one towards Kane, who accepted it without a word.

He scuffed his shoe on the linoleum.

'To Ryan,' David said and drank.

Kane picked at the label on the neck of his bottle.

'You can stay the night,' David said. 'If you need to.'

Kane looked around the kitchen.

'Are you going to stay there? Live there, I mean?' David asked.

Kane chewed his lip. 'I don't know,' he said truth-fully. 'I really don't know.'

When Margaret came into the kitchen, her funeral clothes replaced with a dress that was equally as sombre, they could tell she had been crying. She looked at the beers on the table. 'Coffee?' she asked.

Kane nodded, picked some more of the label off.

'Drugs,' David spat when the coffee had filtered through. He drank some more beer.

Margaret sat a small bowl of sugar cubes on the table. 'Don't, David,' she said. She poured the coffees. 'We shouldn't be worrying about the drugs, whether it's true or not.' She turned, a cup rattling on a saucer in her hand. 'We should be worrying about who killed him. If I get my hands on the bastard, I swear, I'll—'

She stopped, her breathing quick and erratic. She sat the cup down. 'Sugar, Kane?'

—

Sugar Kane. That's what Ryan often called him.

On their anniversary, three months ago, Kane had come home early from work, slaved in the kitchen, laid the table with a red tablecloth and made sure the cutlery and crockery and glassware was just so. He bought a bouquet of flowers to decorate the table, wrapped the gift he had bought for Ryan, and then he sat down and waited.

Half an hour after Ryan should have been home Kane opened a bottle of wine and had a small glass.

Then a large glass.

When he heard the front door open, the bottle was almost finished and his head was fuzzy.

Ryan came in, hanging his head in shame. 'Babe,' he said. He was two hours late.

Kane shook his head. 'Don't.'

'Baby, please.'

Kane stood and took his wine glass to the sink.

'I'm sorry,' Ryan said.

Without turning round, Kane said, 'Where were you?'

'I got caught up.'

'No shit.'

Ryan came a little further into the room, looked at the food on the table, looked at the clock on the wall—after nine o'clock. 'We can heat it up,' he said.

'It doesn't matter,' Kane said.

'It'll only take a minute.'

'Forget about it.'

Kane dried his hands on a tea towel, dropped the towel on the counter, and paused. For a moment, neither of them said anything. Then he turned, his face steely, and walked towards the bedroom. 'Happy anniversary,' he said.

Ryan took his arm and stopped him. 'I'm sorry, baby. It won't happen again.'

Kane closed his eyes, couldn't look at him. 'No excuses, Ryan. If you don't want this, just let me know.'

'What? Where'd that come from?' He turned Kane to face him.

'You've been absent for months,' Kane said.

'Work's been keeping me busy. You know I want this. Us.'

They faced each other, Kane's cold stand-off versus Ryan's puppy-dog sorrow.

'You're always busy,' Kane said.

'It'll change, babe. I promise.' He smiled. 'I'll tell work to give me a break. We can take time off, go away somewhere. London or something.' He rested his forehead against Kane's. 'I love you,' he said. 'You know I do.'

Kane chewed on his lip.

'You'll always be my Sugar Kane.'

And they kissed. They forgot about the food, about the argument. They went, instead, to bed, leaving a trail of clothes behind them as they went.

—

At three-thirty in the morning, Kane woke and walked out onto Margaret's patio, shivering in the late August night. She had insisted he stay the night—demanded, even. The floodlights overlooking the back garden sparked as he stepped out and they lit up the night like the sterile light of day. The pool was covered and hibernating. He doubted anyone had been swimming in it in months.

He breathed in the smell of evergreen. The grounds of the house were lavish. Inside, the home was modernity to the extreme. David Bernhard, a financial adviser for some of Britain's top physicians and lawyers, had spared no expense on his home, his castle. It was state-of-the-art. The outside had been Margaret's doing—the rockery, the shrubbery, the apple trees and the small vegetable plots. She had landscaped the grounds to perfection.

Kane hugged himself against the cold. So that was it; it was over now. Ryan was pushing daisies and Kane had to move on, had to pick up the shattered pieces and start living again. It was impossible.

He stood still and the floodlights winked out. Then he moved again and they came on.

When David cleared his throat behind him he jumped. A bat or a bird fluttered overhead.

'I'm sorry,' he said. 'I didn't mean to startle you.' He rubbed his hands together and stood beside him. 'You won't tell, will you?' he said as he pulled a crumpled packet of cigarettes from his dressing gown pocket. 'She thinks I've given up. I have, really. But sometimes...'

He didn't finish. He absently offered Kane one and he declined. David rubbed his chest as he filled the air in front of them with silver-grey smoke.

'Trouble sleeping?'

Kane nodded. 'Every time I close my eyes,' he began.

'I know,' David said. 'It's a shock.' The cigarette reflected in his eyes as he inhaled.

'Thanks,' Kane said. 'For making me stay the night.'

David nodded and smoked some more. 'Want to talk about it?'

Kane smiled ruefully and shrugged. 'I just wish I was more of a help for the police. I—' His voice was cracking.

'Hey,' David soothed, 'Don't cut yourself up. They couldn't expect you to be a witness. You didn't know it was going to happen. You couldn't have seen anything.'

'The guy was right there,' Kane said. 'I heard the car speed off. I should have looked up. If I'd looked, maybe I could have seen—'

'Even if you got the number plate, the car was probably stolen. There was nothing you could've done. Be thankful your attention was on Ryan those last few minutes.'

Kane sighed. He dug his hands into his trouser pockets. 'I just don't know what to do anymore. How do you move on after something like this? He didn't just die. If he'd been sick maybe I'd have been prepared. I don't know. But he was murdered, David. Murdered by God knows who for God knows what reason.'

'You don't think it was the drugs?' David asked.

Kane thought about the phone calls, the voice issuing threats. Your friend owes me something. I'll be in touch. He thought about the note under his windscreen wiper and about the long silences from Ryan over the last few months, the random disappearances that he was starting to remember. 'I guess so,' he said. 'I'm not sure. I mean, so he was taking drugs. All right. But why kill him for it? Surely you're not going to kill someone who pays you for drugs.'

He paused, shivered.

'Unless he wasn't paying,' he continued. 'Maybe he couldn't pay.' He turned and cupped his elbows in his hands. He was ready to go back inside now. 'Maybe he owed someone a lot of money. Maybe this drug guy—the dealer—maybe he got sick of waiting for it.'

'That's a lot of maybes,' David said, stubbing his cigarette out in a tin he had taken from his dressing gown pocket, 'But it does sound plausible.'

'Does it?' Kane asked.

He wasn't so sure.

Five

'Coffee?' Margaret asked. She moved across the kitchen in a tired shuffle, her head bowed, shoulders drooping. The beige dressing gown she wore looked new, much like all her other clothing, but she carried premature old age as she moved.

Kane smiled sombrely and sat at the breakfast bar with a sigh. 'Black, please.'

She worked on her upper lip with her teeth as she handed him a cup and sat down opposite him, picking at an invisible spot on the countertop. She sniffled, sipped at her coffee, and looked away. Kane could see her eyes blinking frantically as she tried to hold back her tears.

'I think they said it might rain later today,' she offered, steering the conversation in a mangled and pointless direction.

He didn't respond, didn't know what to say.

Margaret returned her attention to the counter, scratching with a fingernail, rubbing with a thumb. She wet her lips with her tongue and sniffled again. 'How are you?' she asked.

He shrugged. 'I'm good,' he lied. 'Thanks for — you know — letting me stay the night.'

Her smile was momentary, obligatory.

'I'm letting David sleep late,' she said. 'He needs it.' She sighed and sat back, her arms useless and every-where — folded, unfolded, at her sides, in her pockets. And then her face dipped into her hands and she wept silently.

Kane bit his lip. How could he comfort her when the only thing he wanted was comfort for himself?

—

Ryan had once introduced him to a friend. They'd bumped into him at a nightclub and Ryan immediately conspired with the guy in a corner before bringing him anywhere near Kane. 'Kane, this is Randy.'

He *looked* randy. Kane thought he was off his head, juiced up on alcohol or drugs or both. Randy shook his hand and grinned yellow teeth.

'He's going to buy us a drink. Aren't you, Randy?' Ryan placed his hand on Randy's shoulder. The music drove through the club like waves of invigorating energy.

Randy looked at Ryan. Ryan looked at Randy. Kane looked at the floor.

'Sure,' Randy said. He bought margaritas and sat at their table, rubbing his nicotine-stained fingers together like he had an itch.

Ryan leaned his head on Kane's shoulder, always one for open displays of affection. He kissed his neck, his teeth touching his skin, his tongue flicking out to taste him. Randy cleared his throat between songs and Ryan smiled.

'Got myself some dancing shoes,' Randy slurred.

'Dancing shoes?' Kane asked.

He nodded. 'You know. Shoes. Like, to dance in.'

Ryan squeezed Kane's thigh. 'Randy wants to dance,' he whispered. 'You don't mind, do you?'

Kane shrugged. Ryan put his tongue in Kane's mouth and he could taste the margarita. They disappeared onto the dance floor and Kane didn't see them for nearly half an hour. His head began to spin and his heart accelerated, thumpthumpthumping inside his chest as though it wanted out. And he didn't know it then, but now he supposed Randy could have slipped something into his drink. Ecstasy or whatever. Something. Or it could have been Ryan.

He gulped at his margarita, the paper umbrella whizzing to the ground as it spilled from the glass. Somebody trampled on it and he cursed. He leaned over to pick it up and nearly fell from his seat. He steadied himself against the table and opened his eyes wide then clenched them, then opened them again. He wondered how many drinks he had had.

He felt light. He felt dizzy. But he felt like he wanted to dance. And his heart was still pounding and he was sweating. And when Ryan came back with his dancing queen Kane stood and smiled and fell.

'Whoa,' Ryan laughed and sat him back in the chair. 'Steady on. Are you drunk?' Kane shook his head and the world went out of focus. Ryan's face blurred into Randy's.

When his heart had slowed to a regular pattern and his sweat had dried on his face, Randy was gone and the music was shooting pains through his brain and Ryan was grinning at him like he owned the world.

—

David put the phone down as Kane and Margaret came into the kitchen from the garden. They were discussing some sort of permanent memorial for Ryan, a tree or a statue.

'Who was that?' Margaret asked, kissing David on the cheek.

'Just work,' he said. He juiced an orange. 'I have to go into the office. Not for long. Are you going to be okay?'

'The office?' she asked, sitting a tall glass flute on the counter for him.

'It's this London deal,' David told them.

'I thought that was cut and dried,' Margaret said.

'You have a deal in London?' Kane asked.

'It's big,' he said. 'A very important client.' He drained the orange juice into the glass. To Margaret he said, 'Something's upset our contact and we need to get it sorted or it might fall through. You'll be all right? I'll only be out for an hour. Two at the most.'

Margaret nodded and smiled distractedly. Her attention was on a framed photograph of Ryan and Kane that hung next to the clock. David knocked back the orange juice, kissed his wife, patted Kane on the back, and left.

'He spends too much time in the office,' Margaret said, still looking at the picture. She took the snap two years ago with a black and white film. It was natural; Margaret hated posed photographs. Ryan was opening a Christmas present and Kane was only half in the frame, half out of focus, watching him. The huge Christmas tree sparkled in star-like kisses in the background.

'It was a great Christmas,' Kane said. 'Ryan never laughed so much.'

'Yes,' Margaret said, her hand held to her breastbone. She turned away, obviously in pain.

'What's this deal David's doing?' Kane asked.

'Sorry? Oh. I'm not sure. I never really understand these things. Some financial thing, I expect. Clematis,' she said. 'That would be nice, wouldn't it? Opposite the apple tree. We could put a little plaque there. You know, with his name on it.'

Kane followed her gaze out into the garden. The apples were ripe. Full of life.

'What do you think?' she asked.

'That would be nice,' he said.

And she cried against his shoulder.

—

Dinner at Margaret's. She said she wanted to be close to Kane, closer than before. She no longer had a son; for nearly four years Kane didn't have a mother. Ryan got him through her last cancerous days, through the funeral, and through the desolate days and months that followed. Now Margaret and Kane were leaning on each other, offering support and receiving it in kind.

David was distant during the meal. He and

Margaret were having a whispered conversation when Kane arrived and as they ate they barely spoke to each other. Kane could only think it had something to do with the outcome of his London deal.

Ryan was the topic of conversation for the most part. 'Remember,' Margaret began, 'the time you saved his life?' She looked at David, smiled wistfully.

Kane had never heard this story. 'When was that?' he asked.

David shook his head. 'Years ago.'

'He could have drowned if it wasn't for David,' Margaret told him. She drank from a glass of water. 'Where were we? Algarve?'

David nodded, chewed some food.

Margaret continued. 'It wasn't long after we'd eaten, I think. We were sitting on the beach and it was so hot. I remember I made Ryan put on twice as much sun block as normal. He went for a swim. I told him not to go too far but you know what boys are like.'

She paused. Kane waited, listening. It turned out he didn't know Ryan at all.

She sat her cutlery down, laced her fingers under her chin. 'He got caught in the tide or something. If it hadn't been for David's keen eye...Well. He rescued him, anyway. Ran into the water, swam out to him, and dragged him back in, coughing and spluttering like he'd swallowed half the sea. It was months before he went swimming again.'

Margaret took another drink and sat the glass down, daubing at the corners of her mouth with a peach-coloured napkin. She gave a tiny burst of laughter, but her eyes remained sad. Everything was just a memory now.

David chewed on his food and stared at his plate.

Kane could see the tension between them was hurting Margaret. He had to ask. 'How are things with your London deal, David? Everything okay?'

David snorted and Margaret took another drink.

'Not good,' he said. 'The bas—' He glanced at Margaret and stopped himself. 'This guy in London has got it in his head that the deal won't work. Says it's just a feeling, but someone must've said something.'

'Any idea who?' Kane asked.

'No, and that's the thing. No one would want to jeopardise this for us. It's a big deal. Our biggest.'

So that was it, Kane thought. David was losing a deal and he and Margaret had argued about it.

But David continued, 'I'm going to have to go over there. Try to rescue the whole situation. I leave tonight.' He shook his head in disgust. That revelation would have hurt Margaret even more than a lost deal. Not long after her son's death and already her husband was talking about going out of the country.

'Isn't there anyone else that could go?' Kane asked.

'Apparently not,' Margaret said.

'Honey, I told you this already. There's no one else we can trust. I thought you understood.'

'What I understand is that you think your work is more important than everything else.'

'That's not fair. You know that's not true. But this deal, it's the biggest thing we've got. If we clinch it, we're set.'

Kane cleared his throat. He wasn't sure if he should try to help them resolve this, or step back out of the way.

'I buried my son yesterday,' Margaret spat. She stood and stared at David. 'You think that was easy for me? What I need right now is some support. I didn't expect you to come home and tell me you're jetting off to London on some business-like holiday.'

David simply stared back at her, his eyes narrow, one hand making a fist around his napkin. Calmly, he said, 'It isn't like that. I love you, Margaret, and I loved Ryan like he was my own, but you have to understand. This business is all we have. If I can't make it work we'll go under.'

Margaret blinked, picked up her plate, and left the dining room for the kitchen.

Kane put his hands on the seat of his chair to stand. 'Should I...?'

'Leave her,' David said. Then he sighed. 'I'll go.'

Kane watched him go through into the kitchen and stared at the door as it swung closed. Their voices were muffled, angry, and then gradually their tone softened and he thought he heard Margaret tell David she loved him. 'Of course I'll come with you,' she said.

When they came back into the dining room he was standing by the CD rack at the far wall holding a copy of an Ella Fitzgerald album. Ryan was a fan. Kane turned as they entered. 'Do you mind?' he asked, holding the CD up.

'Not at all,' Margaret said, her eyes hooded and sad. She came and stood by him as he slotted the CD in, and she read the track listing on the back of the cover.

Ella's profound and sultry voice filled the room as she crooned her happy rendition of Basin Street Blues. Margaret swayed to the rhythm, the CD cover clutched to her chest.

'Ryan couldn't get enough of the oldies,' Kane said. Margaret smiled.

Kane turned as David approached, handing them each a brandy. Ella finished her song and the room lapsed into silence for a few seconds until she picked up the beat with Lover Come Back to Me.

David put his arm around Margaret, kissed her and suggested they retire to the living room before Kane went back to his flat. Margaret had offered to let him stay another night, but he refused. He felt he had overstayed his welcome already. If he was going to step foot back into his life, he needed to do it soon.

Kane drove aimlessly, going nowhere. He knew he needed to reconnect the threads of reality again, but he hated the idea of walking back into his empty flat.

He drove by the cemetery but could not enter. He drove by Ryan's workplace but did not stop. He even drove up the 20mph road outside their old secondary school but he kept his eyes straight ahead, refusing to look at the building, at the playing field, at the grassy spot in the corner where they used to sit at lunchtimes, planning their weekends and their future.

When the last cold rays of sunlight gave up breathing life into the streets of Belfast and the evening became oppressive, he turned the car for home. As he drove, he thought about the possibility of moving house. The flat wouldn't seem the same any more, an empty container with nothing to fill it. He knew all his memories were there, but he could easily pack them up with the furniture and take them with him. A house was just a building. It was love that made a building a home.

There was a mild chill in the air when he stepped out of the car and triggered the central locking system. He walked through the empty parking lot and into the building, picking up the small amount of junk mail from his box.

When he slotted his key in the door and opened it, he was struck by how dark it was. Across the room, the clouds were banking up outside the window. He flipped the light switch and dropped the post on the table. Then there was an immediate and audible oomph and a searing pain at the back of his head.

He fell.

Someone was on top of him. He tried to turn around but was hit on the head again. His right ear rang from the collision. He didn't know what the object was but he was sure it wasn't a hand or a fist.

He tried to shout for help.

'Shut up!' a muffled voice ordered.

Two pairs of hands grappled with his body and roughly turned him onto his back. He could feel a knee on his stomach, just below his breastbone, then a pair of hands around his neck.

His mind was strangely alert as he could feel his lungs labouring for air. The men's faces were hidden in balaclavas. The man on top of Kane, the only one he could see clearly, was wearing a dark green hoodie.

For seconds—minutes even—he struggled against his assailants, and for a moment he thought of Ryan. What would he look like in Heaven?

And just before he blacked out, the room went crimson and purple.

Six

It was pitch black. Even before he opened his eyes he could tell he was in a vast, open space, like a warehouse or something similar. His shallow breathing echoed back across the room. He could feel his hands between his back and the cold floor he was lying on, the rope or twine that held them together cutting deep into his wrists.

It took him a minute to remember what had happened. There had been someone in his apartment, someone strangling him. He swallowed saliva and coughed.

He wondered what time it was. Something told him it was night, something beyond the darkness around him. As he let his eyes adjust to the lack of light, he twisted a kink from his neck and tried to position himself so that his hands weren't pressing into his back so much. Overhead, some fifteen foot above, he could just about make out a corrugated ceiling.

There was a distinct smell of wet and rotting wood that clung to the stale air around him. His stomach churned and, without realising the consequences, his cracked and hoarse voice shouted for help, the words grating in his throat. He lay his head back down and breathed through his nose. There was a soft scuttling noise not far away. A rat, he thought.

Soon he heard a key turn in a lock and a door swing open. The blinding beam of a flashlight fell on his face. He could see nothing, but over the sound of the blood pounding in his ears he could hear footsteps coming towards him. He squinted against the light, the glare hurting his head.

A sharp pain exploded in his hip when someone kicked him. 'Get up,' a rough and surly voice ordered.

Kane tried to move. 'I can't,' he breathed.

The man kicked him again. 'Get up!'

'P-please, I...'

He crouched and gripped Kane's hair. The pain in his scalp was agonising. 'We've got company,' he said evenly. 'I want you on your best behaviour. Now get up.' He pulled on Kane's hair and forced him into a sitting position, then let him go.

Kane's head span. He coughed and twisted his legs around so that he could get some leverage to rise. The man stepped back and watched. Using his hands behind his back, Kane pushed downwards against the sweaty concrete and forced his body up, but he had only risen an inch or two before his arms gave way and he was back on the ground.

The man laughed. 'You faggots are all the same. It's so much fun being tied up, isn't it?' He leaned down and helped Kane this time.

When he was finally standing, weak legged and stomach sore, the man ran the beam of the flashlight up and down Kane's body. The light that splashed back on him revealed his appraising face, harsh angles, narrow eyes. 'You look like you slept on the floor all night,' he said.

He flicked the beam towards the doorway, indicating that Kane should walk. 'Slowly,' he said. 'If you fall again I won't be picking you up this time.'

'What do you want from me?' Kane asked. The

man smacked the flashlight into the side of Kane's head and he stumbled.

'Shut up. No talking. Move.'

Kane shuffled across to the door and was pushed through it, out into a blindingly bright room. He could hear the buzz of the overhead lights.

'He's on his way,' a second voice said.

It took Kane a few seconds to adjust to the new lighting. When he could see again, he noticed two men in the room. One of them wore a green hoodie.

This one, the man from his flat, came up to him, right in his face, and said, 'Not a word. You're going to sit down over here and shut up.' He pulled up his hoodie and showed a gun tucked into the waist of his jeans. 'Any questions?'

Kane lowered his eyes from him and turned his head away. The man took his arm and guided him to a chair where he was told to wait. It still wasn't clear to Kane what was going on. His arms were beginning to ache behind his back, his legs feeling numb and his head hurting.

A short time later, someone's phone rang. The

man in the hoodie stepped out of the room to take the call. When he returned, he pulled his gun out and said, 'On your feet.'

The outer door opened and another man walked in. He was well into his fifties with silvering hair and a pale grey suit.

Without a word, he approached Kane. His smile was cold and sinister.

'Mr Rider,' he said at last, 'glad you could join us.'

Kane kept his eyes trained over the man's shoulder, unable to look at him.

'My name's Lucas Dawson,' he said. 'I told you I'd be in contact.'

—

'I'm going to ask you once,' Lucas Dawson said. 'Then I'm going to kill you.' He motioned to one of the men, who handed him a gun. When he flipped the safety off and pressed the barrel against Kane's forehead he almost fainted. 'Where is it?'

'What?' Kane said. He clenched his eyes. 'Oh God. Oh God, please…'

Dawson pressed harder against Kane's forehead. 'I don't think you heard me, Mr Rider. Did he hear me? I don't think he did. I'm a man of my word, but I'm going to pretend you didn't hear me the first time. Do you know where my package is?'

'I don't—'

Dawson cut him off. His hand gripped Kane's jaw, pressing his cheeks to force his mouth open. When he shoved the barrel of the gun in beyond Kane's teeth, against his tongue, the metallic taste made him retch. He could feel Dawson's breath on his eyes.

Kane whimpered.

There was silence. Or at least he didn't hear anything. With his hand on the back of Kane's head, holding him upright, Dawson withdrew the gun. Kane's legs gave way and he slumped out of the chair and vomited on the ground.

'Put him back inside,' Dawson said, and he turned and left.

Kane was lifted roughly from the floor and hurled back through the door into the darkness. 'Sleep tight,' someone said, and the door closed behind him.

—

The side of his face was numb from where it had been pressing against the concrete floor for the last half hour or more. He worked himself into a more comfortable position against a wall and breathed.

Do you know where my package is?

Dawson's words echoed in the emptiness of Kane's head. He didn't know what he was talking about. He thought—and then immediately discarded the idea—that Dawson had the wrong man. But it was Ryan—he was the reason Kane was tied up in a warehouse with endless possibilities of torture and death. He knew it even before he had seen Dawson. He knew it even as he was being strangled in his flat. He knew it all along.

What had Ryan done? It was bad enough thinking he had been murdered because of drugs, but what else could he have been involved in?

Kane thought back over the last couple of months, searching for any behaviour that placed Ryan at odds with normality.

His mind flashed on the night he died, his limp body in Kane's arms, the apology he breathed before death took him.

Do you know—

Kane rolled down onto his side, Ryan Cassidy shooting hoops with his emotions. He was dead and yet, somehow, he was more alive in Kane's head than ever before.

—where my package is?

He pulled his knees up to his chest. Ryan had stolen something from Dawson. That much was obvious. But why?

Do you know where my package is?

The pain in his heart outweighed the physical pain he was feeling, his wrists torn and bleeding behind his back. No one would miss him.

If it was still night, the night after Ryan's funeral, Margaret Bernhard would be out of the country with David. There was no one else to care about him, no one else to even remember he existed. Ryan's friends were exactly that: Ryan's friends. He was the outgoing one. He was the sociable one. Kane knew some of them, sure, but he wouldn't consider any of them friends. And none of them would come looking for him.

The sound of the men's voices in the next room

was loud, their laughter defiant. For some time Kane listened to what they were saying, unable to make it out or take it in.

And just before he drifted off into a fitful sleep, a mouse scurried across the floor in front of him and he didn't even care.

—

He flinched against the light that spilled across his face as the door opened. A silhouette stood in the doorway, a broad man, a cigarette burning in one hand. Dawson. He took a step inside and was immediately followed by his two cronies, guns drawn and at the ready. Kane didn't move.

Dawson turned and flicked a switch on the wall. Rank after rank of overhead lights buzzed on. Kane saw a mouse scurry into a dark corner and disappear. As he had already suspected, the warehouse was practically empty, except for a stack of old wooden pallets along the far wall. It was perfect killing ground, he thought. God only knew how far from the rest of the world they actually were.

The ground he was lying on was uneven and green with mould in patches. He tried to sit up. Pea-sized rodent droppings were inches from his head.

'No need to get up on my account,' Dawson said.

Kane stayed where he was, his back arched inward, his chin on his chest. 'I don't know anything,' he said, his voice fractured, throat dry.

Dawson nodded and sucked from his cigarette. He came and crouched beside him, his men remaining by the door, eyes ever vigilant, alert to possible threats. It was unnecessary—Kane was completely at their mercy and they all knew it.

Kane blinked.

'Ryan Cassidy,' Dawson began. 'You loved him?'

Kane looked away from him.

'He was a good man, yes?' he continued. 'Very resourceful. Except he didn't know when to quit. So I made him quit. I have this...special power, you see. People tend to do the things I tell them to.'

Kane turned back to him and glared straight in his eyes. 'He can't do anything now.'

Dawson shrugged. 'An unfortunate turn of

events for you, I'd imagine. But, you see, I'm not concerned with the smaller things in life.' He paused. Kane looked away again. Dawson inhaled deeply from his cigarette and flicked some ash on the concrete floor. He breathed the smoke out through his nose before he spoke again. 'I asked you a question a short time ago. Will you give me an answer now?'

For a second Kane thought about spitting in his face and suffering the consequences. If he was going to kill him, it would be better to get it over with. But cowardice overcame him. 'I don't know what you're going on about,' he said.

Dawson was silent for a moment, as if contemplating his words. Finally, he said, 'That's not the answer I was looking for. I stopped playing games when I was six, Mr Rider. Now, I want you to tell me what you know, or Mrs Bernhard might just have a nasty accident.'

He recoiled at the mention of Margaret. Was Dawson holding her hostage, too? What unthinkable acts would he do to her?

'Please,' he begged. 'I don't know anything!'

Dawson pinched the bridge of his nose with a

thumb and forefinger and sighed. In an instant he held Kane's head down on the concrete and jammed his cigarette into his neck.

Kane screamed.

Dawson held the cigarette there, concentration but no effort on his face. When he flicked the cigarette away, the burning sensation continued. He stood, looking down on Kane like a sentencing judge. He sucked his lips and turned away.

'He doesn't know,' he said as he walked out of the room. 'Pick him up.'

'On your feet,' one of the heavies commanded.

Seven

'Get up. Now!'

They kicked him in the side until he worked himself onto his knees, struggling to keep his balance without the use of his arms. 'Please...' he begged. Their guns were inches from his face.

'Fucking faggot,' one of them said.

'Get up,' the other one reiterated.

His heart rate was soaring, thumping against his chest, his throat constricting, a cold sweat itching down his back. He breathed deeply through his nose as, with all the effort he could muster, he drew himself to his feet.

They pushed him out into the anteroom and Dawson walked purposefully towards him. He punched Kane in the stomach and Kane doubled over in pain.

Dawson gripped his hair, pulled him upright again. 'You've wasted enough of my time.'

'Please, I—I don't know anything about—' He could taste bile rising in his mouth.

Dawson punched him again, let Kane buckle to the floor.

'Let's go for a drive,' he said.

His heavies helped Kane up. They gave him something to drink. The water was warm and cloudy but he guzzled as much as he could, spilling more down his chin and shirt than he actually drank. The man who held the bottle to his mouth—O'Reef, he thought he had heard the other one call him—was doing his best to help him drink it. His hands were still tied behind his back.

'Do I have to be tied like this?' Kane asked O'Reef. He didn't answer. 'What time is it?'

He led Kane outside into the cold night air. They rounded the corner of the warehouse and at the bottom of the path was a black hatchback. Its engine was running.

Kane looked around, trying to figure out where he was. A road ran off the drive, but other than that there was nothing, no landmarks that he could use to get his bearings, no road signs. Nothing. An empty field stretched off at either side of the road, electricity pylons extending into the horizon. Were they still in Northern Ireland?

O'Reef took his elbow and walked him down the drive to the car. He pushed him into the backseat, but before closing the door, Dawson came and leaned in towards him.

'I believe you,' he said. 'You don't know where it is. But you're going to help me find it. You have no idea how much pain I can give you. Got it?' He straightened up, walked around the car to the front passenger seat. 'Blindfold him,' he said.

O'Reef took a roll of silver duct tape and stretched a length across Kane's eyes, patting it down so that he could see nothing. 'Move over,' he said and he got in beside him. Kane felt the muzzle of a gun against his neck. 'I like this car,' he said. 'Don't make me get blood on the upholstery. You sit there and keep quiet.'

Kane nodded complacently. With a gun in his face, he was a model citizen.

—

A police officer waved the taxi through and it pulled up at the drop-off point outside Belfast City Airport. The rear passenger door opened and David Bernhard stepped out. He stretched his legs, twisted his head from side to side, and turned, leaning back in to take Margaret's hand to help her out.

Margaret was staring blankly out of the far window. She didn't take his hand.

'Margaret?'

Discreetly, she wiped a tear from under an eye, refused to look at him.

'Margaret, honey,' David said. 'We can't miss the flight.'

'I'm sorry,' she said.

'Sorry for what?'

She looked at him and her sigh was heavy. 'I can't go. I'm sorry. It's too much, too soon.'

'But…'

She shook her head. 'You'll be fine without me. I'll only be in the way. Have your meeting and call me tomorrow evening.'

David looked at the taxi driver, looked back at Margaret. 'This isn't the time for—'

'Grieving?'

He closed his eyes momentarily, and then got back in the taxi. 'I won't go,' he said. 'It was foolish of me. Someone else can do it.'

'No one else can do it. You said so yourself.' She took his hands, smiled at him. 'Go. Seriously. I'll be fine. I'll get some sleep. I just need some time. To heal.'

David tightened his fingers around Margaret's hands. 'Are you sure?'

'Go,' she said. And she kissed him.

David paid the taxi driver double fare to get Margaret home again, and then she watched him disappear inside the terminal building before the taxi pulled away, turning out of the complex to double-back down the A2 the way they had come.

It was the right thing, she thought. David would be home in a couple of days and in the meantime she could try to piece her life together again. The pain of losing Ryan was solid, touchable, as though death lingered with her in the taxi.

—

O'Reef kept his gun trained on Kane for the duration of the journey, its muzzle pressed lightly against his side, just below his ribs. If he tried anything that O'Reef didn't like he could be dead in seconds, so he sat still, leaning uncomfortably forward, his hands still bound behind his back, his eyelashes sticking to the tape over his eyes.

It wasn't too long before the car stopped and O'Reef ripped the tape off. Kane almost screamed with the pain as his skin and eyelids tried to go with the tape. They were parked outside Margaret's house, which looked empty, all the lights out, and the gates at the bottom of the driveway closed. Even now, Kane thought, he couldn't call for help. Margaret's nearest neighbour was over four hundred feet away.

Dawson turned in his seat, pointed at the gates. 'What's the code?' he asked.

Kane looked at the electronic panel outside the driver's door.

'The code,' Dawson repeated.

Miserable, he told him. 'Four, seven, two, four.'

The driver lowered his window and tapped on the keypad. After a second, the gates began to swing open. Ahead of them, the steep driveway resembled a runway, lit at evenly spaced intervals by small, ground-level solar-powered lights.

When the car was parked by the steps of the house, Kane was ordered out. O'Reef stood with him as the driver of the car tucked it out of sight at the rear of the house and he and Dawson returned. The driver put his elbow through a glass pane on the door, reached through and unlocked it.

As they stepped inside, Dawson said, 'Mr Rider?'

The burglar alarm beeped its incessant warning.

'Eight, nine, nine, two,' Kane said, and O'Reef disarmed it.

Dawson nodded at O'Reef who appeared to be Kane's designated keeper. O'Reef pulled a knife from his pocket and cut the cord that bound his hands together. Kane sighed with relief and rubbed at his wrists. They were cut raw.

'I'm trying my hardest to like you, Mr Rider,' Dawson said. 'I'm counting on you to be good. Now, we know it isn't in your flat. As I'm sure you've gathered, we've already checked.'

'Thanks for not trashing the place,' Kane said,

his sarcasm thick.

Dawson smiled. 'My men are superior. They take great pride in their work.' He turned, flicked a light switch. 'But we have no time for that tonight. Darren,' he said to the driver, 'you and our new best friend start upstairs. O'Reef, come with me. I want this place searched top to bottom within twenty minutes.'

The one he called Darren took Kane's arm and shoved him violently up the stairs. Dawson and O'Reef moved further into the living room and began tearing it apart.

Upstairs, Darren pointed to the first door on the left. 'What's in here?'

'David's private office,' Kane said.

Darren opened the door and they stepped inside. The room was sparse. There was nothing but a couch, a desk and chair, and a filing cabinet. On the walls were framed newspaper clippings of David Bernhard with various dignitaries as well as certificates and honours in pride-of-place spots behind the desk.

'Search the desk,' Darren said.

'I don't know what I'm looking for,' Kane said.

'An envelope? A briefcase?'

'You'll know when you see it.'

Darren pulled at the cushions on the couch. It was evident that if the package was in this room — although how Ryan could get it in here without David knowing about it was beyond Kane — it could only be in the filing cabinet. With the couch cushions torn open and discarded on the floor, Darren turned to the filing cabinet. He tried to open the drawers but they were locked. He fished his hand down behind the cabinet and came up with nothing. He nudged it to test how heavy it was.

And then he withdrew his silenced gun and fired a bullet at the lock without warning.

'Jesus!' Kane said, shrinking back.

Ignoring him, Darren opened the drawers one by one, filtering through the confidential files, but he didn't find what he was looking for.

—

They worked their way through the guest rooms without sight or sound of Dawson or O'Reef.

Darren kept a close eye on Kane as they searched first one room, then another, methodically tearing things apart, pulling drawers out, overturning furniture.

When they entered Ryan's old bedroom, Kane felt like he was out of options. If whatever they had been looking for was here, he was pretty sure they were going to kill him and be done with it once they had it in their possession.

This clearly wasn't some sectarian operation by one side of the Catholic-Protestant divide or the other. As far as Kane could figure, this was something altogether more sinister.

'Search,' Darren told him.

Kane tried to protest. This was Ryan's sanctum, not a treasure hunt. 'It won't be —'

Darren nudged him with the point of his gun. 'Move it.'

On the writing desk were several old paperbacks and a few of Ryan's dog-eared schoolbooks—filled, Kane could be sure, with his careful handwriting, blue ink lettering that was all straight ups and downs, serif flourishes on the letter A.

In the top drawer of the desk, as Darren dropped books and electronics from the bookcase, Kane found some of Ryan's childhood artefacts: a Disney pencil case from Florida, a couple of small, plastic crocodile figures, the kind you'd get from a Kinder Egg, and a Gameboy with a couple of old cartridge games.

In the second drawer he found a Swiss army knife and some loose change from various foreign countries. He felt like he was breaking a trust with Ryan. He had been in this room so many times before, but seldom without him and never to snoop.

Kane looked around the room. He could almost feel his presence, hear his laughter, sense his touch. They had shared a lot here. Saddened, he sat back on his heels and sighed. It was no use. As much as he wanted to hate Ryan for what he had done, he simply couldn't.

'Anything?' Darren asked.

Kane eyed the Swiss knife and half-closed the drawer. 'Nothing,' he said.

—

No one could have heard the taxi pull up outside the electronic gates that had closed on near silent pneumatics after Dawson's car and come through them.

Margaret thanked the driver when he had taken her small suitcase from the boot of his car, tried to pay him a little extra but he refused, and then she walked slowly up the long drive to the house.

She was halfway up the drive before the fact that every single light inside the house was on had registered in her mind.

She saw the broken glass panel on the door and hesitated. There was silence from within. She dug her mobile phone out of her purse and dialled 999. 'Police, please,' she said. She spoke with them briefly, then ignored their advice to remain outside the property, and she pushed the door open.

—

Dawson and O'Reef entered Ryan's room. The old man approached Kane and slapped the back of his hand across his face. Kane's eyes clouding with hot anger, his cheek stinging.

'I'm not very happy, Mr Rider,' he said levelly.

Kane stammered. 'I don't know where it is.'

'Shut up,' he snapped. 'I should have had you taken out the same time as your filthy boyfriend.'

He drew his gun.

'On your knees.'

'Please—'

'On your knees!'

Kane looked around at Dawson's men. They were stony-faced and unaffected. He could feel that familiar tightness in his throat and a violent redness in his eyes as he slowly lowered himself to his knees beside the writing desk. His mind was turning somersaults. What can I do? How can I save myself?

Dawson levelled his gun against Kane's head. 'You have one last chance before I decorate the room with your brains. Do you know where it is?'

Kane couldn't speak, his mouth dry, coppery.

Dawson cocked the trigger.

It was then that, like a dream, Kane heard Margaret's voice break through the fear in his head.

'What the hell's going on?'

Beyond Dawson, in Ryan's doorway, stood Margaret Bernhard, rifle in hand, the barrel aimed at Dawson's back as steady as if she was preparing to shoot clay pigeons.

'Don't move,' she said.

Dawson slowly turned to her.

Eight

'Margaret,' Dawson said, his voice calm, his palms upturned in a placating manner. 'How lovely to see you.'

'Shut up,' Margaret snapped. 'Who are you? What do you want?' She edged a step further into the room, the rifle gripped tightly in her hands, its long barrel trained almost professionally at Dawson's chest. 'Kane?' she questioned.

O'Reef held his gun up, ready to fire should his boss give the command.

'We're just conducting a little business,' Dawson said. He frowned. 'I was terribly sorry to hear of your son's demise. Most unfortunate.'

'What do you know about that?' Margaret asked, her eyes darting between Dawson and the other men—O'Reef with his gun pointed at her,

Darren standing almost casually in the corner.

Kane watched as Margaret held firm against the threat of death. He was powerless to do anything, to act in her defence. On his knees behind Dawson, where only seconds before he was about to be shot, his mind ran quick-time, searching for any way out of this.

Dawson shrugged in answer to Margaret's question. 'He was a sweet boy,' he said. 'I liked him. I liked him a lot.'

'I want you out of my house. Now.'

Dawson laughed. Kane couldn't see his face, but he was sure he was smiling. 'I'm afraid we can't do that, Mrs Bernhard. You see, my friend here'—he stepped aside to give Margaret a clear view of Kane in all his fear and pain—'is helping me out. I'm in a bit of a quandary. Your son rather unfortunately stole something from me. Mr Rider was just helping me retrieve it.'

'I don't care what you want. Just get out.' She jerked the rifle. 'I'm not afraid to use this.'

'I'm sure you're not,' Dawson said.

'Let's kill them both,' O'Reef said. Dawson told him to shut up and O'Reef lowered his gun just a

111

little.

'Kane, get up,' Margaret said.

'That's not advisable,' Dawson retorted.

Kane didn't move.

The small, black gun in Dawson's hand lolled as though he had forgotten it. 'If you'll kindly let us get on with our work,' he told Margaret, 'the sooner we'll—'

'My husband is—'

Dawson cut her off with a chortle. 'Your husband is in England. You should have been with him.'

'That shows how much you know,' Margaret said, her voice as steady as her hands. 'He's downstairs calling the police.'

'We both know that's not true,' Dawson said. 'Why aren't you with him?'

'I'm a woman,' Margaret said. 'I'm allowed to change my mind.'

Dawson grinned. 'How is David these days?' he asked. 'Still taking time out to play squash?'

Margaret looked confused, her head twitching slightly.

'Oh, yes,' Dawson scoffed. 'He and I go way

back. Years, in fact.'

Kane was just as confused as Margaret was, but Margaret had quickly composed herself.

'I don't believe you.'

'He was never any good on the golf course,' Dawson said. 'But on the squash court, you'd never tell he was a man in his fifties.'

Margaret shook her head. 'Get up, Kane.'

'Silence!' Dawson shouted.

A shot went off and everyone ducked, followed immediately by another shot. Kane rolled forward, head dipped, shoulder taking the brunt of the fall on the carpeted floor, and knocked against the side of the desk.

He saw Margaret and Dawson both fall away from each other, Margaret's body slamming against the doorframe, Dawson hitting the back wall.

Kane reached into the drawer and pulled out the Swiss army knife, extended the blade, and lurched over Dawson as O'Reef raised his gun. He jabbed the knife forward, into O'Reef's chest, knocking his firing arm off aim as he spat off a round. The bullet glanced off Kane's shoulder, tearing skin and spewing blood. Simultaneously,

Kane pushed upwards with his other hand against O'Reef's chin. His head bounced off the wall behind him and he fell, the knife still in his chest.

Margaret, bleeding from the stomach, weak, her face distant, fired point blank at Darren before he had time to react. His face exploded as he went down.

Kane turned, a cold sweat on his face, and saw Dawson slumped against the wall in an oddly wretched sitting position, his legs outstretched, spread-eagled. A lopsided grin played on the left half on his mouth. The first shot he had heard must have been from Margaret.

Breathing hard, he watched as Dawson gurgled, something between a laugh and a cough. 'Margaret,' he said, his voice thick, clogged.

Remembering Margaret, Kane dropped to the floor beside her. 'Margaret? Are you all right?' he asked.

Dawson gurgled again.

'Margaret, listen to me,' he said.

Margaret's head turned, her eyelids closing and opening in a painfully slow blink. She looked at Kane. 'You're bleeding,' she whispered.

He touched his shoulder, pulled his hand back. He hadn't felt the pain until she brought it to his attention.

'Mah-gret,' Dawson choked. His arms flopped to the floor at his sides, his fingers loosening around his gun. He wheezed as he breathed. 'You think...it's over,' he said. His half smile returned. 'It isn't.'

And then he was silent. Kane thought maybe he was dead. But his eyes flickered and his bloodied tongue protruded to moisten his lips.

Margaret pushed her shoulders back and winced. 'Why,' she tried, stopped, started again. 'Why do this?'

Kane took her hand.

Dawson breathed. 'If David could see us now, eh?' His words were interrupted by a fit of coughing, blood running down his chin to his suit jacket.

Kane watched Margaret blink, the name of her husband almost lost on her. She tried to say something, then stopped.

'Ryan had something,' Dawson said. He had let go of his gun completely now, his fingertips coiling in towards his palms. 'Something incriminating. Something David wanted back.'

His head drooped forward and he whispered, 'Documents. Damaging documents.'

Kane twisted onto his knees, one hand on Margaret's shoulder. 'Why are you telling us this?' he asked Dawson. 'Why now?'

'You think...I care?' he said. 'I owe nothing to David Bernhard.' He coughed blood onto his shirt.

Margaret choked.

'Why did you have to kill him?' Kane asked. 'What'd he ever do to you?'

Dawson's head turned just a fraction to look at the prostrate form of O'Reef, the small Swiss knife protruding from his chest. 'You've...had your revenge,' he said.

He looked at his gun on the floor beside his hand. 'Kill me.'

Kane rose, kicked the gun away. 'Tell me what Ryan took from you. What was it?'

Dawson didn't move. His eyes were glazed.

Kane crouched beside him. 'You said Ryan had documents. What documents?'

When Dawson said nothing, Kane gripped his

shirt and twisted. But there was no reaction; Dawson was dead.

'K-Kane,' Margaret breathed.

He turned and rushed to her side, dropping to his knees, reaching out for her but afraid to touch her. The gunshot wound in her stomach looked ripe and crimson.

'Margaret.'

He patted his pockets but couldn't find his phone. He shuffled over to Darren's faceless body and searched his pockets, gagging as his hands were covered in blood. He pulled out Darren's phone and called for an ambulance.

When he hung up and dropped the phone, Margaret said, 'Who—?'

He soothed her. 'Don't. Don't talk. It's okay.'

She closed her eyes. Kane thought he could hear sirens already.

A deep guttural sound came from her throat. She opened her eyes and looked at him. 'Kane…'

'It's okay,' he said again.

'Prom…Promise me,' she said, her voice a whisper. He had to strain to listen to her. 'Don't let them res…resuscitate me.'

He blanched. 'Margaret, no—'

She twisted uncomfortably. 'Yes. If I...die. Please. Don't let them resuscitate me. Promise.'

Kane was crying. 'Please, Margaret. I can't.'

Margaret reached up and feebly clasped his hand. 'Promise me,' she said.

His lips trembled. 'I can't do that.'

'Promise me.'

He looked away, clenched his eyes, bit his lip. 'I promise.'

When he looked back at her, she had her eyes closed. Shallow intakes of breath made her throat rattle. He kept hold of her cold hand. 'They'll be here soon,' he said. 'Don't worry. They'll be here soon.'

In the moments of silence that followed, he was reminded of the last time, just recently, that he was kneeling beside a dying person. Ryan resembled his mother so much that it was hard to look at her without seeing his face, the eyes, the shape of the nose, the curve of the lips.

Margaret pushed her tongue out between her lips and quickly drew it in again. She looked up at him. 'Kane...' she said, her voice a rasping whisper. 'David is…in London.'

Blood glistened on her shirt.

'I won't let you die,' Kane exhaled, his own voice sounding strange, distant.

'Damaging documents,' Margaret said as though to herself. Her fingers gripped tighter around Kane's hand. 'Find him.'

'What?'

He could hear the whistle of ambulance sirens getting closer.

'Find out…what he's doing.'

'Margaret, I—'

'Stop him. Whatever it is.' She paused, breathed. 'I never…I didn't…' She choked. Kane waited as she caught her breath. 'Stop him,' she said again.

'I will,' Kane said. 'I'll stop him. Look, the ambulance is here.' Someone was pounding on the front door.

'Don't leave me.'

'I'm not leaving. Just hang on, okay?'

She released her grip and he got to his feet, the pain in his shoulder forgotten. He stumbled down the stairs, opened the door and let two paramedics and some police officers in.

'She's upstairs. Quick!' he yelled at them.

When they got to her side, Margaret looked dead.

Nine

His arm stung and his fingers were numb but the bullet hadn't done any lasting damage to his shoulder. They stitched him up, put his arm in a cloth sling, and prescribed some painkillers. And now, in a family room in the hospital, two police officers sat opposite him and wrote down the lies he told them.

'So let me get this straight, Mr Rider,' the taller of the two officers said, notebook in hand, pen tapping against the arm of his chair. He had a cropped brown beard and large, penetrating eyes. 'You went to Mrs Bernhard's house—you said you were sleeping with her son?'

Kane looked at him. 'I said I was her son's boyfriend.'

'Yes. Right. And now he's deceased. Stabbed?'

'You don't believe me?' he asked, looking from one to the other. 'Call the station. Speak to Detective Thorpe.'

'We believe you,' the talkative officer said. 'We just need the facts.' He paused, looking back over his notes. 'So, you go to Mrs Bernhard's home and—what?—let yourself in? Because she wasn't home?' Kane nodded. 'Where was she?'

'Where was who?' Kane asked, although he knew. He was stalling, thinking.

'Where was Mrs Bernhard before she came home?'

'She was supposed to be going to London with her husband.'

'What changed her mind?'

'I don't know,' Kane said.

'Did she come home because she knew the men would be waiting for her? Was that her plan?'

'No.' Kane's voice rose at the accusation. 'She didn't know them, had nothing to do with it.'

'Nothing to do with what?' the officer questioned.

'Nothing to do with whatever they were looking for.'

The officer paused. 'Okay,' he said at last. 'So, these guys rock up, Mrs Bernhard comes home unannounced, and everyone starts shooting each other. Is that right?'

He shrugged. 'Yeah. Pretty much.'

'Pretty much,' the officer repeated, writing it down. 'What were they looking for?'

Kane dipped his head into his one usable hand and said, 'I don't know.'

'I see. And you never saw these people before?'

He shook his head. The officer flipped his notebook closed and they stood.

'Mr Rider, I'm sure I don't need to remind you that perverting the course of justice is a very serious crime. When forensics gets through with the scene, we'll want to speak to you again. We have your details.' They walked towards the door, and then the bearded officer stopped and turned back to Kane. 'You know how lucky you were?' he asked. 'I've seen some nasty shoulder shots in my time. Torn tendons and ligaments.' He touched his own shoulder. 'Shards of bone lodged in muscle tissue. Nasty. Really nasty.' He adjusted the hat on his head. 'Another quarter inch,' he said, 'and that baby would have taken your shoulder clean off, believe me.'

He sat by her hospital bed and held her hand. When he had left her side to let the ambulance crew into her house, she had not died, merely passed out. She had lost a lot of blood, they told him later, at the hospital, but they would perform a transfusion and, in the young Asian doctor's words, 'She'll be back to her old self in no time.'

'Don't let her hear you calling her "old",' Kane had said.

When the police had finished interviewing him he returned to Margaret's bedside and sat vigil while she slept off the anaesthetic. Occasionally he removed his sling and worked some life into his arm, or paced up and down the room to stop the pins and needles settling into his legs. Mostly, he just sat there and watched the monitor beside the bed as it traced her heart rate in a constant fashion. She'd be fine, they had told him. They had removed the bullet and the internal damage, while traumatic, would heal in time.

Find him, she had asked him as she lay bleeding on Ryan's bedroom floor. Stop him.

David's involvement with Dawson, whatever that might be, was a mystery. Perhaps, Kane thought, Dawson had been making it up to frighten them at the end. If David and Dawson were in cahoots, then surely David himself would have searched his house for the missing documents, unless Dawson was double-crossing him. There was no need for the guns and the violence.

Find him. Stop him.

Kane took Margaret's hand again, squeezed it gently, and whispered, 'I can't do it, Margaret.' He lowered his head, pressed his forehead against her hand. 'Whatever David's done…I just can't. I don't have it in me.'

If David was involved, Kane reasoned, he'd most likely have more hired guns at his disposal. How was Kane—twenty-four years old, barely an adult—supposed to stop him? What could he do?

He watched the trace of her heart rate as it drew across the oscilloscope's screen. 'I won't do it,' he

said.

He sat in silence, watching the slight rise and fall of her chest, watching as nurses came in to check on her.

Later, when she was awake, he continued to hold her hand.

She was weak, her voice like gravel. 'It's his birthday next month.'

Kane nodded. He had been planning Ryan's birthday present for months. 'What kind of bastard kills a twenty-five year old?' he asked.

'The evil kind,' Margaret said.

She closed her eyes and rested for a while and he dozed with his head on the bed beside her.

He woke when she touched his hair. He wasn't sure how long he'd been asleep. 'You okay?' he asked.

She smiled, touched his forehead, his temple, his cheek. 'He loved you so much,' she said.

He leaned his face against her hand.

'And I know you love him, too,' she said. 'It's in your eyes.' When he looked up at her, she said, 'I don't care what they're saying. About the drugs. We know him better than that, right?' Kane sucked his lower lip into his mouth, a comfort action, and she continued, 'No, honey, don't look so sad. We need to put our feelings to rest now.'

'To rest?' he asked. 'Forget all about him? Forget the last eight years of my life? Margaret, we were sixteen when we met. That is my life. I can't pick up the pieces from this. He was everything to me.'

'That's not what I'm saying. We'll always have our memories,' she told him. 'But we can't let the past cloud the future. God knows it's not much of a future, but it's all we've got.'

'Ryan doesn't have a future any more,' Kane said, petulant.

'But he does,' Margaret said. She reached out, touched Kane's chest. 'In here. You'll never forget him. I doubt he'd ever want you to. But in time it'll get easier. I don't want you moping around. Keep Ryan in your heart, but don't lay your own life aside. I've already lost Ryan's father. Now this. We have to be there for each other now, you and me. We have to get by or there's just no point.'

A nurse entered before Kane could respond. He knew the wisdom in her words, but it would be easier to speak them than perform them.

'Time to change your dressing, Mrs Bernhard,' the nurse said.

Somewhat forcefully, but polite, Margaret said, 'Can you give us a minute, please, love?'

The nurse frowned, looked from Margaret to Kane to Margaret again. She nodded, said, 'Two minutes,' and then left them alone.

Kane stood, yawned.

'I asked you to go to London earlier,' Margaret said. 'Will you do it?'

He stared at her. He was surprised she had remembered.

'Go back to the house,' she said. 'In the nightstand by my bed there's a...' She lowered her voice. 'There's a small derringer.'

'A what?' Kane asked.

'A pistol,' she said. 'David bought it for me a few years ago but I never used it. Get it and take it with you.'

'Margaret, I—' Kane said, and then the nurse returned. 'I'll wait outside,' he said.

As he stepped out of the room, Margaret called after him, 'Don't forget, Kane. We have to be there for each other.'

—

In the morning, after little sleep, Kane called into work, checked that it was all right for him to stay off for an extra day or two. His boss was understanding. 'Take all the time you need,' she said. 'If you want anything, just let me know.'

He got in his car even before breakfast, filled up on fuel, and drove to Portstewart, to their beach.

When he got there, he sat in the car for some time, staring out at the ocean. He wasn't sure why he had come. Maybe in an attempt to feel Ryan's presence. Maybe in an attempt to forget him.

He got out of the car and ambled over the sand dunes, walking down towards the shoreline. It wasn't exactly beach weather, a brisk wind kicking sand around, and the beach was practically empty.

He pushed a hand into his jeans pocket, sighed deeply and stared out across the choppy water. A lone windsurfer rode the waves.

In one fluid movement, he was sitting on the sand, his legs crossed, his hand out of his pocket and both now hugging his elbows.

He watched the windsurfer flip over a wave in

the distance.

His shoulder was still painful, but not unbearably so. He removed the sling and worked his arm up and down. How long had it been since he last sat here with Ryan? No more than a few months, he guessed.

A young kid came along the beach, dangling at the end of a dog lead. The dog, large, loping, bounded towards Kane.

The kid stopped, looked at Kane as the dog sniffed around him. 'What's wrong with your arm?' he asked.

Kane kept his gaze out across the water. 'I hurt it,' he told him. The dog was nuzzling its wet, sand-crusted nose against his neck.

'How come you're sitting there on your own?' the kid asked.

Kane ruffled the dog's fur, his eyes sad. 'Because I have no one left to sit here with me.'

'Bummer,' the kid said, and he yanked on the dog's lead and walked on along the beach.

Kane, alone again, pulled his legs up and wrapped his arms around them. There was no one left. Ryan was dead, Margaret was in hospital, and

David was God knows where.

The kid had disappeared over a dune.

And the windsurfer had crashed and burned.

—

Margaret Bernhard had always been a tender and loving person. Kane could remember his first encounter with her as though it were yesterday, not long after Ryan had moved to his school and turned Kane's world upside down.

Margaret was pruning a bush as they came up the drive.

'What's for dinner?' Ryan had asked after dutifully kissing her on the cheek.

'I haven't decided yet.'

'Can Kane stay?'

Margaret had looked up at Kane, a twinkle in her eyes. 'So,' she had said. 'You're the young man I've heard so much about.' She pulled a gardening glove from her slender hand and motioned for him to shake. Her grip was firm, her eye contact steady. Kane felt as though he was under intense scrutiny. 'You make sure you keep my boy smiling, okay?'

she said. 'I want nothing but happiness for the both of you.'

The words were so heavily laden with innuendo that Kane did a double take with Ryan to make sure she knew no more than she had to know. Ryan was feigning inattention.

When Margaret had let Kane's hand go, he pushed them deep into his pockets and smiled awkwardly at her. She turned back to her gardening and he and Ryan had walked the rest of the way to the house.

'What was all that about?' Kane asked.

Ryan had shrugged and said nothing. He was smiling.

'What does she know?' Kane asked.

'Nothing,' Ryan said. He continued towards the house.

Kane looked back over his shoulder. Margaret busied herself among the flowers.

From behind him, Ryan said, 'She doesn't mind.'

'Doesn't mind about what?'

Ryan had laughed. 'About...stuff.'

He smiled again and, after a second of processing it, Kane had smiled back.

When he returned to his flat, mid-afternoon, he took a beer from the fridge and sat on the floor of the living room with a box of Ryan's things.

His shoulder was stiff, but he worked as best he could, sifting through Ryan's papers and books and gadgets, most of which had been packed up for years since they moved into the flat—they had little enough space as it was.

He didn't really know what he was looking for, or why he was looking for it. Whatever 'damaging documents' Ryan had stolen, whether they were from Lucas Dawson or from David, Kane was sure that if Dawson's men had already been through the flat, what luck was he going to have?

He drank from his beer, sat the half-empty bottle up on the coffee table beside him, and pulled out another sheaf of papers from the box in front of him. Bank statements dating back years; nothing out of the ordinary. He found a photo album of their formative years that Ryan had pieced together. Childhood photographs of two young boys, growing up on opposite ends of Belfast, growing up side by side in the album, Kane on the left pages, Ryan on the right, until at last they met and every new photograph in the album contained two teenagers, holding hands, arm in arm, laughing, smiling, kissing.

Ryan was the sentimental sort.

Kane sat the album aside after flicking through it twice. When his bottle was empty, he got another beer and another box of memories.

An hour and a half later, five empty beer bottles beside him, boxes of Ryan's life upturned all around him, Kane stood and worked some life back into his legs. There was no more beer in the fridge.

He pulled a storage case from under the bed and pulled it into the living room. It was filled mostly with paperback novels and more photographs that had never made it into albums. In the side of the case was Ryan's pocket digital camera. He had two cameras—a Canon with extra lenses and filters and external flashes, and the little compact Pentax that Kane now turned over and over in his hands. He had rarely used it. 'You can't get a feel for the camera,' Ryan had often said, 'if you can't grip the lens.'

Kane switched the Pentax on and began flipping through the photos on the digital screen. As he suspected, there weren't very many photographs on the memory card. Shots of him and Ryan in various places, various poses. The occasional artistic and abstract shots of lampshades and curtain rails.

There was a blurred image that Kane couldn't quite make out, followed by another blurred shot. The next one was still blurry, but clearer: a few men outside a building. Using the controls on the back of the camera, he zoomed in on the photo but was unable to make out who the men were.

He got up from the floor and jacked the camera into his laptop, downloading the photos to a folder on his desktop and opened the relevant photo. On the larger screen of the laptop, he was able to recognise all four of the men.

Lucas Dawson was centre frame. Behind him, his two goons, Darren and O'Reef.

And beside Dawson, shaking his hand, was David Bernhard.

―

Kane stared at a grainy printout of the photo. It sat next to his strong, black coffee on the kitchen table. He needed to clear his head after the beers.

When he called the hospital to check on Margaret, they told him she was asleep. He enquired about her condition. 'Doing well,' they said. 'Shouldn't be too long before she's able to go home.'

'That's great,' Kane said. 'If there's any change, you'll call me?'

'You've nothing to be concerned about,' they said. 'She'll be right as rain.'

'Great, thanks.' He was about to hang up when instead he said, 'Oh, when she wakes...Tell her not to worry. I'm going to do what she asked.'

A few minutes later he had switched his laptop back on and had entered his credit card details on an airline website for a flight to London. He didn't have a clue what he'd do when he got there, let alone how he'd actually find David, but he had to try. Now that he had proof of David's involvement with Dawson, albeit a grainy photograph, proof that Ryan was killed for a reason, he had to try.

He packed a small suitcase, carefully tucked the photograph of David and Dawson down the side of it, and took one last look around his flat. He stared up at the Bette Davis picture on the wall, chewed on his lip. And he turned and left.

—

'Tell me,' Ryan had said. He was drunk.

Kane smiled, teasing. 'Tell you what?'

They were both drunk.

'Tell me everything. Tell me you love me. Tell me you'll always love me. Tell me…Tell me I make you smile.'

Kane laughed. 'You make me smile. And I love you. And I'll always love you.'

'And tell me,' Ryan said, eyes blinking, head inclining to the left, a lop-sided smile on his face, 'tell me how much I mean to you, 'cause you know I need it. Say something nice.'

'"Something nice."'

'No, seriously,' Ryan laughed.

Kane made a pretence of thinking about it. He

trailed his hand down Ryan's arm and wove their fingers together. 'You know what you mean to me, Ryan. You know how much I love you, how much I need you. The moment you walked into my class, God, my heart—it was pumping so fast I thought it was going to explode.'

Ryan smiled.

'And,' Kane continued, 'you didn't have to come and sit next to me. There were plenty of other seats in the class. But you did. You sat beside me. I could have kissed you right then. Look at me.' He touched his chin. Ryan looked at him. 'I love you, Ryan.' He kissed his forehead. 'I need you.' He kissed his neck. 'God, I love you.'

And he had pulled Ryan into a tight embrace, his arms around his neck, Ryan's hands on the small of his back. Their chests—pressed together—rose and fell in opposites as one breathed in, the other breathed out, like they were yin and yang, like they were a true unison, working together.

And he whispered against his cheek, 'I'd do anything for you, Ryan. Anything.'

PART TWO

LONDON

Ten

He can't find him.

He looks everywhere. In the toilet, at the bar, on the dance floor. He is nowhere, as though he has just disappeared.

A body presses against Kane on the dance floor. He steps away, repulsed. 'Have you seen Ryan?'

'Who?'

'Never mind.'

He pushes through the swell. Why did he have to disappear like that? He scours the faces before him. A fat woman dances in front of him, white powder caked in her nostrils, a wild look in her eyes.

He presses on. 'Ryan?'

His voice is lost in the din. The music pumps. The floor vibrates.

Sweaty bodies gyrate before him, each dancer a

solitary battleship in a violent sea, swaying against the onslaught of music, hands in the air as though in prayer to the god of dance. Energized men bounce around the floor, their upper bodies clothed in nothing more than the glossy sheen of perspiration, their shirts tucked into their back pockets like tails.

And then he is behind him, carrying a drink in each hand. 'Kane! Where'd you go?'

'Where'd you go?' he shouts over the noise.

'The bar. I told you.'

He takes the glass Ryan offers him, drinks it in one gulp. 'I'm tired,' he says. 'Let's get out of here.'

'Wait. One more dance. Come on.'

Ryan kisses him.

'This music's killing me,' Kane offers.

Ryan laughs. 'It's great. It's retro. Let's dance.'

He takes his hand.

'I'm tired.'

Ryan frowns, puppy-doglike. But he holds his hand and they head for the door. And Ryan, on the way out, pats the doorman on the backside. 'Same time next week, sexy,' he says.

The doorman laughs. Ryan laughs.

And the cool night air feels refreshing. It was too

stuffy inside. It was too close.

'Where to?' Ryan asks.

'Home?'

'Party.'

'Home.'

Ryan shrugs. He kisses Kane's cheek. 'You're the boss,' he says.

And a man comes out of nowhere. Bumps into Ryan. Says, 'Sorry, mate.' Walks on.

Kane thinks Ryan is tugging him, pulling him in a new direction, out into the road. And he is suddenly heavy. And his hand comes free from Kane's. And he is spinning — spinning like he is still dancing, spinning like he is still having fun.

But he stumbles. He falls.

And Kane watches him. And he sees the blood. And he sees his face. And Ryan says sorry.

He says sorry.

Kane snapped his eyes open.

He hadn't dreamt of that night since it happened. He had had other, nicer dreams, but not of Ryan's murder. Perhaps it was his brain's way of accepting it as fact.

He had fallen asleep not long after checking into the cheap hotel, stretched across the bed, fully clothed, mobile phone in his hand. The phone had slipped from his fingers in sleep and had fallen to the floor. He picked it up, worked a creak from his neck, and pulled his laptop from its case.

Finding David was his priority, though he had no idea where to start looking. Central London hotels looked like his best bet but you couldn't just rock up and ask if someone was a guest there. Hotel employees were like doctors when it came to confidentiality, he assumed.

He searched for hotels on the laptop and called the first one on the list.

'Hi. Yes, I'd like to leave a message for one of your guests but I'm afraid I've forgotten his room number,' he said. When the girl on the phone asked for the guest's name, Kane said, 'David Bernhard.' He spelled the surname and they answered in the negative. 'Oh, really? I'm sorry, I must have the wrong hotel.'

This was going to be a long and arduous

process, Kane thought, but he would stop at nothing for the outcome he deserved. He dialled the next hotel on the list.

'Hello, can you put me through to one of your guest's please? He's called David Bernhard.'

Again he received a negative response and he quickly moved on.

Almost an hour later, when his arm was hurting from holding the phone to his ear and he thought he'd worn a patch on the carpet from where he paced up and down, he gave up. Did he really think he could find David in a city of millions? It was hopeless.

He called the hospital back in Belfast and spoke to Margaret for a few minutes, assuring her he was fine, ensuring she was fine, and then he showered and changed. He needed to get some air, some lunch.

Outside the small hotel, the sky was overcast and the street was murky. He looked both ways, consulted the pocket guide book he'd picked up from the airport, and went in search of a tube station.

When a black Transit van pulled up and crawled

along beside him, he gave it only a cursory glance and carried on. And when the door slid open and a man on the street took his arm, he still didn't connect the two.

'This way, Mr Rider,' the man said, leading him towards the van.

'What? Get off,' Kane said. 'Who the hell are you?'

The man, stocky, tall, thinning hair, bundled Kane into the van and jumped in behind him. 'Drive,' he said to the guy behind the wheel, and he told Kane to sit.

One side of the van was taken up by computers and other electronic equipment. Another guy sat at a terminal wearing headphones. He looked at Kane momentarily, then returned to whatever it was he had been doing.

'What's going on?' Kane asked.

But they didn't acknowledge him.

—

Thoughts of Dawson had flipped through his head, awful memories of being taken from his flat and dumped in a warehouse. The men in the black van remained silent throughout their journey. The rear door windows had been blacked out, and through the front of the van, one street looked the same as the next to Kane.

They pulled into the back of a large but nondescript building and drove down into the underground car park. When the van came to a stop, the man who had taken Kane off the street opened the door and ushered him out. Their footsteps echoed as they crossed the car park to a lift, the man's hand on Kane's arm the whole time, and they rode up to the third floor.

He was pushed into a room and the door was locked behind him.

Alone, he looked around. There was a desk protruding from one wall of the small white-walled room, four chairs around it, two on either side, and a recording deck sat at the inner side of the table.

He sat down, because there was nothing else to do, and noticed a video camera watching him from the ceiling, its small red light blinking at him.

After a few minutes of silence, the door opened

and a man and woman entered. The man was the same one from the van. He had put a tie on and appeared to have combed his hair. The woman was dressed in a grey skirt suit with a white shirt and her hair was tied back from her face. They sat down opposite Kane.

There were no introductions.

'What are you doing in London?' the man asked.

'You're police?' Kane asked.

'What were you expecting? Why are you in London?'

'You just snatched me off the street,' Kane said. 'I thought you were a bunch of nut jobs.'

'Answer the question,' the man said. 'What are you doing in London?'

'Am I under arrest?'

'I'm asking the questions.'

Kane repeated, 'Am I under arrest?'

'No,' the woman said. 'We'd just like to ask you a few questions. Then we'll see what happens after that. How old are you, Kane?' she asked.

The fact that they knew his name registered only vaguely with him. 'Twenty-four,' he said.

'Been to London before?' the woman asked.

Kane folded his arms. 'Thought I'd come and stalk the Prince of Wales.' He looked at them both. 'Is this some sort of terrorist thing? I don't even know how to spell IRA, let alone how to make bombs.'

'Very funny,' the man said. 'We've been watching you, Mr Rider.' For a moment Kane thought he meant they had been watching him from the camera while he sat there in the interview room, but when the brevity of what he had said sunk in, Kane simply blinked and looked at him. 'Got yourself in a bit of trouble back home, didn't you? How'd you do it?'

'Do what?'

The man smiled. 'Lucas Dawson,' he said. 'AKA Connor O'Leary, AKA Thomas Davis.'

Kane felt the blood drain from his cheeks and his face must have visibly whitened because the corner of the man's mouth twitched in a satisfied smirk. He drew circles on the paper in front of him, moving the pad around, holding the pen in one place, like he didn't have a care in the world.

Kane's throat was tight, his chest burning. Absently, he touched his shoulder where O'Reef had shot him. He was no longer wearing the cloth sling, but it still ached from time to time.

'How's the shoulder?' the man said. 'I hear you flirted with a bullet.'

Kane's vision clouded and he clenched his eyes. 'Who are you?' he asked, his voice barely a whisper.

'UK NCB,' the man said.

'We're from the National Central Bureau of Interpol,' the woman told him. 'Part of the National Criminal Intelligence Service. We've been tracking Lucas Dawson and his associates for some time.'

'What do you want with me?' Kane asked. 'You want to lock me up for killing him? Well, you can't. That pleasure lies with someone else. But believe me, if I'd had the chance, I would have. He murdered my...He killed the only person I ever really loved.'

The woman nodded and they both stood to leave. When they had reached the door, the man turned back to face Kane. 'I'll be honest. I don't get that whole gay thing,' he said. 'Never have. Probably never will. But Ryan—he was one of the good guys. It was a real shame when he died.'

And then they left him on his own.

—

He was numb. His fingers were tingling and his head was spinning. They knew Ryan. That was the one thought turning over and over in his mind.

When they both returned, hardly ten minutes later, Kane was still sitting in the same chair, in the same position, staring at the table top in front of him.

They sat without speaking, and they waited.

When Kane looked up, he asked 'What is all of this? Who are you?'

'Detective Superintendent Wilson,' the man said. 'Pat Wilson. This is Detective Ann Clark.' The woman smiled warmly at Kane and Wilson continued, 'Now, I'm going to ask you a couple of questions, and this time I'd like some answers.'

'How do you know Ryan?' Kane asked.

'What brings you to London?'

'Did you meet him in Belfast? He's never been to London.'

'Why are you in London?'

'How do you know him?' Kane retorted.

Detective Wilson sighed. 'Answer the question, please.'

'You answer my questions,' Kane said.

'You're not in a position to argue with us, Mr Rider. Answer the question or you'll be spending the night in an eight-by-eight cell.'

He stared at Wilson, incredulous. 'Fuck the cell. You sleep in it. If you know something about Ryan, I want to hear it. Tell me how you know him and then I'll answer your questions.'

Wilson was about to say something but Ann Clark put a hand on his arm to stop him. She smiled at Kane again. 'Kane, Ryan Cassidy was working for us, doing us a favour.'

'Working for Interpol?'

'Not the way you're thinking,' she said. 'He wasn't an officer. He wasn't like a secret agent or any of that Bond stuff.'

Kane waited, hopeful of an explanation.

'Ryan...He stumbled onto something. He was just a civilian, shouldn't have gotten mixed up in it, but he did. He approached the PSNI who got the

UK NCB involved, as well as our men in France.'

'France?'

She ignored his question. 'We knew to some extent what was going on, but the evidence Ryan brought to us—well, it was pretty conclusive.'

'When did you meet him?'

'NCB sent us out there. We met with him a couple of times. There were questions we needed answering. Ryan was our only chance.'

She paused, cleared her throat. 'Things were getting tense. Ryan was in way too deep. It was getting out of hand. We were getting ready to pull him out when—'

'When he was murdered,' Kane said. 'Whatever you got him into got him killed. And now you want me to answer your damn questions? It's your fault he's dead, your fault that Dawson kidnapped me, almost killed me, shot Ryan's mother who didn't have any part in this, and now you want me to sit here and play cops and robbers all day?' He was shouting but he didn't care. 'You murdered Ryan,' he said.

'We didn't—'

'It's your fault,' Kane repeated. Had he gotten it

so wrong? Ryan wasn't to blame for any of this. He was murdered because of Interpol.

Pat Wilson scraped his chair out from under him and stood. 'Let's call it a day,' he said.

They put him in a little bed and breakfast in the middle of a terrace block not far from the station. The room was small and airless, sparsely decorated, a single bed with multi-coloured sheets against one wall, en suite shower cubicle, a window that didn't open but let the noise from the street below in anyway. The overhead bulb buzzed like a wasp in a glass jar.

'It's only marginally bigger than a cell,' Clark said when she had checked him in and walked him up to the room. 'But believe me, you'll be more comfortable here. We'll talk again in the morning and if we need you any longer we'll see about swinging you an upgrade.'

'I had a hotel,' Kane said.

She nodded. 'This place is...better.'

He knew what she was implying; this B&B was

under their surveillance.

Clark handed him the room key. 'I hope I don't have to remind you not to do anything rash in the middle of the night, like taking off. Seriously, you don't want to get Detective Wilson upset.'

Kane looked around the room. He was at a loss—about pretty much everything in his life right now.

'Well,' Clark said. 'Good night, then.'

When she turned to leave, Kane said, 'Did...' Clark stopped, looked at him. 'Did Ryan ever...?' He didn't finish the question, didn't want to know the answer.

She smiled. 'Yes,' she said. 'All the time.'

Once she had gone, Kane sat on the bed, leaning against the wooden headboard, and pulled his knees up to his chin. Outside, a car sounded its horn, one long, droning hum splashing around his head, and a motorcycle sped by. His world was crashing again and he couldn't hide from it.

Ryan was...what? He was inside his brain, racking up old memories, rattling though the wardrobe of chained-up emotions.

There were still so many unanswered questions.

And he decided, there in that tiny little room, there in the darkness of night, that he wasn't going to leave London until he had answers to them all.

Eleven

In the pale grey light of early morning, with office-bound traffic already filling the street outside the B&B, car horns and engine sounds penetrating the tiny window in some kind of osmotic ooze, Kane felt out of his depth, as though he was treading water three miles off shore with rapidly tiring legs.

He sat on the edge of the small bed in his underwear, face buried in his hands, as the pintsized kettle on the desk in the corner of the room came to the boil. A plastic cup and complimentary sachet of instant coffee lay beside it.

The kettle shook and rattled violently before switching itself off and he rose laboriously, tearing the sachet open and tipping the granules into the cup. Minutes later, he was staring out the window at the slow-moving traffic below, the cup of instant nestled in his hands. He blew on it and felt the steam rise against his eyes, hot and humid.

There was a brisk rap on the door, followed by the rattle of a key in the keyhole.

Kane turned, coffee in hand, as Ann Clark entered the room carrying his suitcase. She saw him in his underwear and quickly turned to face the door, her hands shooting up to shield her face. 'I'm sorry,' she said.

He laughed and blushed at the same time. 'Don't worry about it,' he said. 'You're not my type.'

Clark turned back to face him, offering a tight-lipped smile. 'Present for you,' she said, placing his suitcase on the bed. 'We had someone swing by your hotel last night.'

She unzipped the case, flipped it open, and pulled out some clothes for him. The contents had already been messed with.

'You've been through it,' Kane said.

'Of course.'

The photograph had been in there. 'Find anything?' Kane asked.

'Nice pair of Mr Men boxers,' she said. 'Get dressed. Meet me downstairs. Continental or fry?'

Kane held his gaze on the suitcase. If she'd found the photo, she clearly wasn't giving anything away. 'If continental means better coffee than this,' he said, placing his cup on the desk, 'let's do that.'

—

As they stepped out of the cheap hotel into the cool London morning, Kane sighed heavily. 'Freedom,' he said. 'I can't believe you're letting me walk free. No handcuffs?'

Clark pointed along the street and they walked at a slow pace. 'You were never under arrest, Kane.' She clutched her handbag under one arm and held her phone in her other hand, either forgotten or glued there.

'Are you always this professional?' Kane asked, digging his hands deep into his jacket pockets.

'Professional?' Clark queried.

'Curt. Abrupt.'

She gave a half-shrug and said, 'You're in a

chirpier mood this morning.'

'Am I? I had time to think about things last night.'

'Cheap B&Bs can do that to a person. What've you concluded?'

It was Kane's turn to shrug. 'Ryan is dead,' he said. 'I can't change that. And so is Dawson, or whatever other name he goes by. That much I don't want to change. But there are still a lot of questions and I want to find the answers to them. I need to.'

Clark pointed to a small, clean-looking café and said, 'Let's eat here. I have a few questions myself and I'm hoping to get some answers, too.'

Kane settled at a pine-top table by the window and stared out at the London buses and taxis while Clark ordered some all-butter croissants and a pot of coffee. When she returned to the table and sat opposite him, the smile she offered was one that implied she was ready to talk business. Kane pinched his lips together and waited for her to get down to it.

She went straight for the punch. 'What aren't you telling us, Kane?'

'What makes you think I'm hiding something?'

'That response tells me that. Let's not forget,

Kane, in your words I'm professional. I'm good at what I do and what I do is read people.'

Kane pursed his lips, leaned back in the chair.

'You think I'm full of it,' she said.

'No, I think I'm not the only one hiding things.'

Clark pushed a stray strand of her shoulder-length brown hair back behind her ear and refused to look away from him. If she was good at reading body language, she was even better at hiding her own.

The silence stretched on until Kane couldn't take it any more. 'What do you want me to say?'

'Tell me what you know,' she said.

Kane paused, turning away from her and looking out the café's window. 'Last time I spoke to the police, I was taken from my flat and locked up in a warehouse and shot at.' He looked back at her. 'What makes you think I want to go through all that again?'

'What have you got to lose?'

His short burst of laughter was cold. 'My life,' he said. 'I may have lost everything else, but that's one thing I'd still like to hang on to.' He pulled his coffee closer to him and stirred some sugar into it.

'Tell us where he is.' Her voice was verging on

impatient.

Kane looked up at her again. 'Who?'

She shook her head. 'Kane, we have to stop playing games.'

'This stopped being a game when I held Ryan in my arms and watched him die.' His voice was flat. The elderly Greek man behind the counter was watching them, dusting down the countertop like he had nothing better to do.

Ann Clark sat in silence for a moment. Then she said, 'Tell us where he is. Tell us what you know.'

Kane ran a hand across the back of his neck and clenched his eyes. The world around him was going blurry.

'Tell us what you know,' she repeated.

He drummed his fingers on the table and for a full minute neither of them spoke. Then, finally, he said, 'Shouldn't you be taping this or something?'

—

Pat Wilson scraped his chair in as he sat at the interview table next to Clark. He leaned his elbows on the table, wrapped the thick fingers of one hand over the fist he had made of the other and pressed his thumbs against his chin.

Clark reached out to press record on the tape deck.

'Wait,' Kane said. She stopped, her finger hovering over the button, and looked questioningly at him. 'What's going to happen to me? Once I tell you what I know. Are you going to let me go? Lock me up?'

'That all depends on what you tell us, Mr Rider,' Wilson said.

'But it'll go no further, right?' he asked. 'Whatever I tell you, it'll stay between us?'

'This is not a confessional booth, Mr Rider. Do we look like priests?'

Clark said, 'Whatever information you provide will be held in strict confidence. Of course, if it's pertinent to our investigation, we'll have to discuss some things with our team. But your name will never be used outside NCIS and the local authorities.'

'Which authorities?'

'We're an international organisation,' Wilson said. 'Our role is to coordinate and advise. Our work depends on local forces as well as partnership with foreign agencies. We operate within the mandate of the NCIS and the General Secretariat in Lyon, France. Whatever information you give us—'

'Relevant information,' Clark cut in.

'—will have to be passed on to the appropriate authorities. In this case, the Command Centre in Lyon and the Metropolitan Police here in London.' Wilson sat back in his chair. 'Press the button,' he said to Clark.

She glanced at Kane momentarily, and then pushed the button. 'Commencing interview, twenty-first July, six minutes past ten. Case reference KR-681-E. Persons present, Detective Superintendent Patrick Wilson, Detective Ann Clark, and interviewee.' She turned to Kane. 'For the benefit of the tape, can you please confirm your name?'

'Kane Rider.'

'Thank you,' Clark said.

Kane shifted uncomfortably in his chair.

'Let's start with why you're in London,' Wilson said.

Kane looked at the cassette recorder as the tape reel wound in its casing. For a moment, he couldn't speak. Then finally, hoarse, he said, 'I was looking for someone.'

'Who?'

He stared up at Wilson's surly face. 'I think you know who.'

Clark sat forward. 'We'd like you to tell us who you're referring to, Kane.'

'Why?'

'To show we're not leading you.'

He looked down at his hands. 'I was looking for Ryan's step-dad. David Bernhard.'

'Good,' Wilson said. 'Now we're getting somewhere. Why were you looking for him? What made you suspect he was in London?'

The questions were relentless. Wilson and Clark acted almost like a tag team, hitting him with question after question and barely giving him enough time to think. He figured it was their usual style—give a man enough time to think about his answer and you give him enough time to come up with a lie.

They asked him about David Bernhard, about Lucas Dawson, and about Ryan and even Margaret. It was clear they knew more about Ryan than Kane did. How much of his life had he kept from him?

They stepped up the interview a notch when Wilson asked, 'What do you know of Bernhard's involvement with Lucas Dawson and the murder of Ryan Cassidy?'

The room was stifling. Even Wilson had loosened his tie.

Murder. It sounded so surreal.

So real.

'Nothing,' Kane said. 'Before Ryan's death, before this whole mess began, I didn't know a thing. I didn't know David was involved in anything. I never would have suspected him if it wasn't for Dawson.'

The detectives sat in silence, waiting.

'Before Dawson died—when he was shot—he told us Ryan had some damaging documents that implicated David in something. I'm not sure what. I don't know anything about any damn documents.'

'And when you found Bernhard?' Wilson asked. 'What then?'

Kane shook his head. 'I don't know. Talk to him. Nothing makes sense any more. Ryan's dead. David was there for him. How could he be a bad guy in all of this? He loved Ryan. I don't get it.'

Wilson nodded and opened a paper file. He picked out a clear evidence bag that contained the photograph Kane had had in his suitcase and he slapped it on the table in front of him.

'I am now showing Mr Rider a photograph taken in evidence from his personal belongings,' Wilson said for the tape. 'Where did you get this?'

Kane glanced at Clark. 'It was on one of Ryan's cameras. I guess when Dawson searched my flat he was looking for printed documents, not photos.'

'Do you know any of the people in this photograph?'

Kane nodded.

'We need to hear you, Mr Rider,' Wilson said. 'For the tape.'

'Yes,' Kane said. 'This is David. That's Dawson.'

Wilson pointed at the photo. 'David who? Does he have a surname? That could be anybody.'

Kane closed his eyes. 'Bernhard,' he said. He thought it had been obvious. 'David Bernhard.'

Indicating the other men in the photo, Wilson said, 'And these two?'

'Dawson's men,' Kane told him. 'O'Reef and somebody.'

Clark said, 'Noonan. Darren Noonan and Mike O'Reef.'

Kane pushed his chair back a few inches, rested his elbows on the table and put his face in his hands. He was tired.

Wilson checked his watch. 'Okay, Mr Rider, let's have five minutes. Interview suspended at eleven twenty-six.'

—

A few months ago, when spring was slowly giving way to an early summer, Kane and Ryan had spent the weekend at Margaret's while she and David were in Dublin on business.

They had eaten an early dinner and drank a bottle of wine, and they had taken a second bottle out to the pool as the sun was tumbling down behind the distant horizon, their jeans rolled up to their knees, feet wading in the cool water.

They lay down and watched the first stars appear and Ryan made a wish. He leaned his head on Kane's chest and said, 'People are confusing.' He was being philosophical.

'You're confusing,' Kane laughed.

'I know. That's my point.' He unfastened one of the buttons on Kane's shirt and slid his hand inside, cold fingers against Kane's warm stomach. 'I wish I was psychic,' he said.

'Why?' Kane asked.

'So I could know what people are thinking.'

'I thought being psychic meant talking to the dead.'

'You know what I mean,' Ryan said. 'I could be a mind reader.'

Kane wrapped an arm around Ryan's shoulders. 'Whose mind would you read? There's not much in mine that you don't already know.'

'I know everything I need to know about you,' Ryan said. 'But think about all the other people in the world. Who knows what they're thinking, what they're about.'

'You'd want to read their thoughts just to find out?' Kane asked.

'Wouldn't you?'

'I don't think we need to. I think what makes us human is the fact that we can get to know people in so many other ways.'

'But you never really know them,' Ryan said. He

sat up, sighed, took another drink from his glass. 'Fuck it,' he said, and that was that, subject changed. 'Get your kit off,' he said.

They laughed like naughty children as they stripped naked and jumped in the pool, and they swam lengths side by side and splashed each other and Ryan let Kane take him at the shallow end.

Later, lying next to each other on a blanket, shivering in the night air and holding each other tight, Ryan said, 'You know I love you, don't you?'

'Do you? I thought it was just lust.'

Ryan slapped Kane's naked thigh. 'That too,' he said, then he pinched his lips together. 'You touch me in ways no one else ever has.' When Kane was about to say something witty, Ryan slapped him again. 'If you're going to be like that,' he said, 'you can bite me.'

'I already have,' Kane laughed.

Ryan stood and pulled his jeans on.

'Hey, babe, don't be like that.'

'It's okay,' Ryan said. 'I'll get another bottle of wine and then I'll kick your ass.' He crouched, kissed Kane deeply, and went inside the house.

Kane put his hands behind his head and stared up at the night sky. Ryan's philosophical moments weren't just alcohol-induced. Lately, it seemed he could fade out of the real world into his mind without any notice or warning. Kane often had to repeat a question before Ryan would acknowledge him. It wasn't so much a distance as a detachment, Kane thought, like he was pondering the laws of the universe.

Ryan was right, Kane thought. People are confusing.

—

After another hour of questioning, Wilson left Clark to finish up. When she took Kane through all the paperwork, she walked him to the front of the building and showed him out.

'So you're just letting me go?' Kane asked.

'Go home, Kane,' she said.

'What am I supposed to do?'

'Get some rest. You look like you need it.'

He thought they all looked like they needed it. 'But...Dawson,' he said.

'Yeah, off the record? Thanks for that.'

'I didn't do it.'

171

'You were part of it, though.' She sighed. 'We were planning on bringing him in. That's the official take. Unofficially, I'm glad he's off the streets and not tying up our hands.'

'David was his boss?' Kane asked.

'Associates,' she told him. 'Dawson worked for many people but was bossed around by none.'

Kane watched her as she put her hands in her pockets and stared down the street. 'And what about David?' he asked.

'We have it in hand. We'll find him.'

'If he had something to do with Ryan's death, I want to destroy him. Stab him the way Ryan was stabbed.'

She touched his shoulder. 'If ever we need you to do that, I'll get in touch.'

Kane looked around. 'I can't believe this is it. After all I've been through, this is it?'

'Listen,' Clark said. 'Hang up your spurs, cowboy. Your involvement stops here. Leave it to the professionals, okay? Don't go chasing bad dreams. If you pursue this, I will arrest you.'

Her mobile phone started ringing and she unhooked it from her belt.

'I'm sorry,' she said.

Kane flatted his lips together. 'Yeah,' he said. 'Me too.' And he walked away from her.

—

She watched him walking down the street and felt sorry for him. She knew it couldn't have been easy for him, coping not only with the death of his partner but also the revelations that followed.

She brought her phone to her ear. 'Clark,' she said.

Wilson sounded like he was out of breath. She could hear his footsteps on stairs. 'I've just spoken to the guys on the street,' he told her.

'What's happening out there?'

Kane was almost out of view now, his shoulders slumped, his gait slow and meaningless.

'They've found him,' Wilson said, referring to Bernhard. 'He's on the move.'

'Where is he? Where's he headed?'

'They're tailing him now. He's going west.'

'On his own?' Clark asked.

'He's with three other men. One they recognise. The other two are just shadows. Intel has it

Bernhard knows someone's in town.'

'Rider?' she asked. How could he possibly know?

Wilson said, 'Bingo. I want him disappeared.'

There was another voice on the phone then, someone passing by. 'Not now, Dixon,' Wilson said. 'I'm in a hurry.'

Clark laughed. 'Kick him for me,' she said. 'He still owes me for that bet last month.'

There was a brief exchange between Wilson and Dixon before Wilson said to Clark, 'I want him in a safe house.'

'I've just let him go,' Clark said.

'You've what? Get him back.'

Clark started running down the street before he'd even said it. 'I'm on it,' she said and she ended the call.

Twelve

Kane was walking the few short streets back to the B&B so he could pick up his things and think about heading home again when he heard, some distance behind him, Clark's voice calling his name.

He turned towards her and saw that she was running as fast as she could.

'Kane!' she shouted again. She stopped in front of him, not even remotely out of breath. 'You've got to come back.'

'What?'

'Bernhard's on the move. He knows you're here.'

'How?' Kane asked. He looked around the street as though David would come strolling up towards him at any minute.

When they got back to Interpol Headquarters, Clark led him up to Wilson's office. As he sat in one of the chairs in front of the desk, Wilson was on the phone. 'Just keep me posted,' he was saying. 'Stay on him.'

He slammed the phone down and Clark asked, 'Where?'

'What's going on?' Kane asked.

Wilson ignored him. To Clark, he said, 'Embankment. They're still moving.'

'Who's his tail?'

'Mickey Brown,' Wilson said. 'He won't lose him.'

Kane watched the exchange between the two detectives, only half able to follow the words. How could David know he was in London?

Wilson looked at him, sighed. 'You have no idea what you've got yourself into, have you? We'll put you in a safe house, away from harm. Bernhard won't find you.'

'He's actually looking for me?' Kane asked.

'Dawson's dead and the news is out. He knows his wife took a hit, too.'

'What's he doing now?' He looked from Wilson to Clark.

'Coming after you, no doubt,' Wilson said.

Kane shook his head. 'Why isn't he going home?' he asked. 'If he knows Margaret's in hospital—'

'He's too shrewd for that,' Wilson told him.

'But he loves her.'

'Collateral damage,' Wilson said. 'If he does love her, he'll send her flowers when he's finished his business here.'

Kane stood and curled his fingers into fists. 'You still haven't told me what's going on.'

'Sit down,' Wilson said.

Clark said, 'It's best if you don't know.'

—

The safe house, a ground floor flat in a nondescript street in Central London, was run down but serviceable. It was one of eight houses that Interpol currently utilised throughout London and the Home Counties, under authority from the Met. In truth, it appeared more of a storage hold than a welcoming home, but as Clark opened the door and allowed the afternoon sunlight to fill the living room, dust mites dancing in the air current, she nodded almost to herself, and said, 'It'll do for now.'

Kane and PC Burton—lending a watchful eye from the Yard—stepped in behind her.

'You really think he's coming after me?' Kane asked, looking around at the flat.

'You want to take that chance?' Clark said. 'Burton, put the kettle on, will you?'

'Yes, ma'am,' Burton said and went to the small kitchen off the living room.

'You can't keep me here,' Kane said.

'It's for your own protection.'

'You said I wasn't under arrest.'

Clark pulled a dust sheet from the sofa and dropped it in a corner. 'You're not,' she said. 'But we still have the power to hold you. I can arrest you if it makes you feel better.' When Kane was about to protest, Clark added, 'Look, we'll take Bernhard out soon. Until then—'

'Take him out?' Kane asked. 'Kill him?'

Clark smiled ruefully. 'No. If only we had the authority to dispose of the bad guys, our job would be a hell of a lot easier. He's too important to have him in a body bag.'

Kane sat on the sofa and picked at a thumbnail. 'The man's a bastard,' he said. 'How could he keep this secret life from everyone?'

Sitting down beside him, Clark said, 'Everyone's got secrets, Kane.'

'Drugs,' Kane said.

'Excuse me?'

Kane shook his head. 'Ryan had a secret. He was jacking up on heroin and I didn't have a clue.'

Clark looked away from him, chewed her lower lip.

'What?' Kane asked. She ignored him, adjusted the cuffs of her jacket sleeves. 'What?' he said again. 'You can't tell me he wasn't doing drugs. I saw the coroner's report.'

She looked at him. 'Kane.'

'Tell me.'

Clark stood, sighed, walked away from the sofa to the old gas fire in the brace wall, and walked back to him as she spoke. 'It's true they found heroin in his system during the autopsy. And yes, he was injecting. But it wasn't what he wanted. Not that.'

'It never is, is it?' Kane said. 'But I didn't know. How could I not have known?'

'He did his best to keep it from you.'

Kane stared at her, looking up from his seated position. 'How well did you know him?'

Clark sighed again. 'NCB have been in contact with him for nearly six months.'

'Six months?' The idea that Ryan had been involved in this subterfuge for so long both shocked and confused him.

'He was a good asset,' Clark said. 'He shouldn't have been, but he was.' She sat back down beside him, watched his face. 'The heroin...It wasn't his fault. You have to understand that.'

'Go on.'

'Jesus, I'm going to lose my job here,' Clark said. She pinned a strand of hair behind an ear. She looked towards the kitchen, making sure Officer Burton was still out of ear shot, and she lowered her voice. 'I'm only telling you this because—look, I'm doing you a favour. You have a right to know.'

Kane kept quiet, listened intently.

'About four months ago,' Clark said, 'Bernhard knew Ryan was on to him, but he didn't know how deep he'd gotten.'

'How deep did he get?'

'Deep enough,' she said. 'Listen to me, Kane. David Bernhard had Ryan injected with it. With the heroin.'

Kane closed his eyes and listened to her voice as

she told him what Ryan had relayed directly to her—the warehouse, Dawson, O'Reef, the heroin. When they knew he was getting too close to their dirty little secrets, they accosted him, strapped him into a chair in that dank storage unit in the middle of nowhere, tied a shoelace around his bicep to lock his veins and reveal them under the gloomy overheads, and stuck a needle in his arm.

Ryan had screamed, tried to thrash about, but they had tied him down and gagged his mouth. And they stood back, Ryan had told Clark, stood back and watched as he tripped off his face. He was dizzy, tingly at first, but a rush of warmth quickly consumed his whole body and his brain was buzzing and alert and he felt euphoric, he felt alive.

And the funny thing, Ryan had said, the absolute funniest thing, was that he could have sworn David Bernhard was standing in a recess, in the shadows, watching and smiling and smiling and watching.

And he felt alive.

And he felt fit.

And he felt happy.

When Kane opened his eyes again there were

tears on his lashes. 'Why?' he breathed. 'Why give him heroin?'

'To get him hooked,' Clark said. 'To stop him chasing their tails. He wouldn't grass on the one man who could...'

'Make him feel happy?' Kane asked, sensing the irony. 'Make him feel alive?'

'Drugs are like that, Kane. That's not who he was and you know it.'

'So this whole thing,' Kane said, 'all this shit — it's all about drugs?'

Clark shook her head. 'The drugs were just a side line.' She glanced at the kitchen again, realised Burton must have heard at least part of their conversation and was staying out of the way, and she said, 'It's weapons, mostly. This is one of the biggest cartels we've ever seen, operating out of more than twelve countries. Mexico, Peru, the US, UK, Spain—'

Kane stood. 'Ryan was killed because of drugs and guns?'

'No,' Clark said. 'Ryan was killed because of Bernhard's greed.'

'He loved David.'

'But he didn't trust him. Not at the end. He

knew too much. The heroin was a way to put him off, get him addicted so that he needed Bernhard to keep supplying it. We were arranging rehab.'

'But why?' Kane asked. 'Why get him hooked on drugs? Why not just kill him when they found out he was on to them?'

'We could speculate forever,' Clark said.

'And you,' Kane accused. 'Why didn't you stop it? Why'd you let him get addicted instead of pulling him out and saving his life?'

'We didn't know. He didn't tell us about the drug-taking until it was too late. This is not a blame game, Kane. We did what we could with the information we had.' She stood and touched his arm. 'Believe me, if there was any other way, if he had told us from the start, we'd have fixed it. This is Bernhard's fault. Ryan wouldn't have started on the heroin if it wasn't for him.'

Kane nodded, resolve in his eyes. 'You have to let me help. I can get close to him. Reel him in or something.'

Clark shook her head. 'I can't allow that. He knows you're here and he'll know we've got you. You're not friendly any more. I've told you before, let us deal with it.'

'I can't just sit here and wait for it to be over.'

'If you don't just sit here,' Clark said, 'it will be over—for you. I'm sorry, Kane, but there's nothing you can do.'

They faced each other, staring hard, anger and frustration flashing between them.

When Burton came back into the living room, carrying a tray of mugs and a teapot, the movement at his peripheral vision broke the spell and Kane relented. He said, 'I want my boyfriend back.'

'I know,' Clark said. She touched his arm again. 'I know.'

Thirteen

As Clark entered Interpol's headquarters that afternoon she was determined that this whole fiasco would end now. She owed it to Kane, owed it to Ryan. They had been sitting on this mess for long enough; it was time to act. The organisation to which David Bernhard belonged was escalating its operations both here in the UK as well as in France and Africa. If the guys in Lyon didn't pull their fingers out soon, Interpol might miss the only chance they might have.

Arms dealing was big business on the continent. Bernhard's organisation had no name—not officially, anyway. On the face of it, they operated under multilateral treaty laws and the trading of guns and ammunition was not, in itself, illegal. What they flouted were the UN Security Council's arms embargoes. Clark, Wilson and the rest of the teams entrusted with international safety measures could do little to stop the arms trade, short of enforcing import-export laws.

But the arms business was simply a cover for global drug smuggling. Why they had decided to share these two cargoes, Clark could only ever hazard a guess. But to her, in light of the evidence they had amassed recently, Bernhard's associates clearly hoped that if they were stopped for their arms activities they would get a slap on the wrist and their baseline drugs operations would continue unhindered.

Taking down those acting illegally on UK soil — Bernhard, Dawson, the handful of others that NCIS had been following for some time — was not the full extent of Clark's duties. Putting an end to the worldwide business was their ultimate goal and one she hoped they would achieve soon before anyone else should die unnecessarily.

She swiped her pass card at a turnstile and headed towards the bank of lifts on the far wall. She had left PC Burton with Kane in the safe house, with a promise of coming back later with food.

When Detective Jim Dixon hurried up with a toothy smile and walked along beside her, she said, 'You owe me money.'

'Give me a chance to win it back,' Dixon said.

'In your dreams.'

'Got your guy in a house?'

'Got your own cases to be working?' Clark asked.

'I get the boring cases,' Dixon said. 'Tell Adams I want in on yours.'

Clark pressed the call button for the lifts. Dixon was one of those unfortunate individuals with sharp weasel features and the stature of a tunnel-dwelling troll. At five-foot-very-little, if it wasn't for his wisecracking tongue and his apparent desire to bathe in cheap cologne, Clark assumed he could enter a room unnoticed and remain there undiscovered indefinitely. Despite his appearance—or perhaps because of it—he had a string of women constantly on the go. Clark would never have believed it if she hadn't seen it for herself. Whatever desire he aroused in these women, she failed to see it herself.

'Wilson would never allow it,' she said in reply to his request.

Dixon pressed the call button after Clark had done so and stuffed his hands in his trouser pockets. His tie had been done up wrong and ended about three inches below his belt. 'Adams'll tell him,' he said. 'Come on, you want me on your team, don't you?'

'As much as I want your nuts for breakfast.'

Dixon sucked air in through his teeth. 'Play fair,' he said.

Tired and irritable, Clark said, 'What do you want, Dixon?'

He looked her up and down. 'I want to play with the big boys.'

When the lift doors opened, they waited as half a dozen people got out, and then they stepped inside.

'The case,' Dixon said. 'You can get me in. Come on, let me help. I'm going mad stuck up there with Biggs and his doughnuts.'

'Get out of my lift, Dixon,' Clark said as she pressed the button for the third floor.

'Your lift?'

'My lift,' she said, and she pushed him out just as the doors closed. You could only manage to listen to Dixon for an extremely short period of time. If he wasn't begging to be on bigger cases — he was currently working a national auto-theft case, a classic cut and shut outfit—then he was delighting everyone with the intimate details of his sexual conquests.

Up on the third floor, she walked down the corridor to Wilson's office and found him at his computer.

'They've gone into some gentleman's club,' he said without looking up. 'We can't get in without blowing cover. We're watching the exits.'

'Bernhard has a penchant for expensive brandy and upper crust politics?'

'Fuck knows,' Wilson said, cracking hard on the keyboard.

'What's he up to?' Clark asked.

'You've got him in Six?' Wilson asked of Kane.

'Safe as houses,' Clark said.

Outside the office, Dixon was hovering in the corridor as though he intended to say something. He appeared out of breath from using the stairs. Wilson motioned for Clark to close the door and when she had done so, Dixon could be seen through the window mouthing his disgust at being excluded.

'We're going to have to make a move on Bernhard before he gets to our new best friend,'

Wilson said. 'We let Ryan Cassidy down. We can't lose another.'

'Losing Ryan wasn't our fault,' Clark said.

'You don't believe that.'

She frowned. 'No.'

Jim Dixon hurried to his workstation cubicle, bypassing Lucy without comment. He'd say something later, something about that new top she was wearing. He could roll the quips off his tongue like a dog drools over a bitch in heat. He was that close to bagging Lucy at the Christmas party last year, if it hadn't been for DCI Adams and his protective arm. Adams had to be pushing the limits of retirement and treated the girls on the force like each and every one of them was his favourite niece.

Dixon had to watch what he said around Adams. Interpol detectives weren't above the long arm of the law any more than were the criminals they pulled off the streets, and Adams was fit for slamming on someone most mornings. Dixon kept his kiss-and-tell dialogues until the old man was out of ear shot. He worked the basement for four months the last time Adams overheard him bragging about the fit bird that yanked him outside a pub.

He settled at his desk, looked around, and woke his computer out of sleep with his control card. He phoned up to Biggs and asked for the file reference for their witness on the cut and shut case.

'What for?' Biggs asked.

'Just give me the damn reference, Biggs, I don't have all day.'

He tapped the reference key into the computer and brought up a list of possible actions. He clicked protection state on the screen and then clicked property locale. He couldn't access the safe house list without a case reference. The nature of the new data system meant that every click and keystroke was recorded with Central Data Housing on the top floor. If he was questioned about it, he'd allude to the possible need for protection status for their auto-theft witness following allegations of death threats, which wasn't entirely unlikely.

A list of safe house locations numbered one to eight filled his computer screen. The system was circumspect, offering only the information one was entitled to see. Dixon didn't have the authorisation to release full house details but there was enough information on his screen for him to glean what he needed to know.

Of the eight houses, only two were marked in-occ, short for In Occupancy. Having heard Wilson mention House Six to Clark, and seeing its in-occ status, he pulled up the details for the residence.

The screen flashed case specific classified, and below that were the words 'Occupant Protection Detail'. At the bottom of the screen, the house's address was listed along with Pat Wilson as the authorising signatory.

Dixon glanced over his shoulder, caught sight of Lucy's legs under her desk, and then turned back to the screen. He picked up his personal mobile phone and dialled a number from memory.

When a man answered his call, Dixon said, 'Got him.'

Fourteen

Kane took a shower in the small bathroom in an attempt to clear his head. The world had gone fuzzy and he needed to scrub himself of recent revelations. As he stood in the bath, the shower curtain sweeping out and sticking to his legs, the hot water cascading over his face, he was reminded of standing in the rain one evening with Ryan and feeling as though all their cares were being washed away, as though they were being cleansed.

They had been out for dinner that night, straight after work, still in their suits, and hadn't had too much to drink. The weather had turned sour earlier that week and there was little sign of it ever letting up. In the back of the taxi on the way home, Ryan had loosened his tie and put a hand on Kane's leg. The driver kept his eyes straight ahead. Full of dim sum, Kane felt content and at ease with the world.

Outside, the rain was driving hard and the taxi's wipers were on full power.

As they turned a corner and drove alongside a dark and deserted park, Ryan cleared his throat and said, 'Pull over here, mate, please.'

'What?' Kane asked. 'Where are you going?'

'Shortcut,' was all Ryan said as the taxi pulled to a stop. The driver put his interior light on.

'What are you talking about? It's pissing down out there.'

Ryan paid the fare on the meter and gave a generous tip. You always knew when it was Ryan's payday.

'I'm going to give you a sense of adventure if it kills me,' he said.

Kane looked out into the dark storm. 'It'll kill us both.'

Ryan opened the door, took Kane's hand and pulled him out into the cold rain. He pushed the door closed and waved the driver off.

Kane hunched his shoulders and squinted against the sting of fat droplets on his face while Ryan spread his arms wide and lifted his face towards the sky.

'It's like heaven's tears,' he said.

'It's fucking freezing,' Kane retorted.

Ryan looked at him, grinned. 'I'll warm you up later. Come on.'

He took Kane's hand again, led him towards the park entrance. The gate was open but the park was empty. 'No one in their right mind,' Kane said.

'Who wants a right mind? Live a little.'

Stooped and chilled through, Kane allowed himself to be guided along the path. 'You'd better not be taking me cruising.'

Ryan laughed. He let go of Kane's hand and ran out into the middle of the grass near a fountain. He threw his arms in the air and screamed with such delight that Kane could only smile and roll his eyes. The rain beat on him like nettles. 'Come on,' Ryan called to him above the din.

'Never,' Kane said.

'Get your arse over here, now.' It was a comic command, not meant harshly. 'If you love me, you'll join me.'

'I have to get wet to prove I love you?' Kane asked. He held a hand over his already soaked hair and laughed as he watched Ryan.

Ryan didn't answer. He held his mouth open to catch the rain.

'If that's acid rain,' Kane said, 'it'll kill your insides.' He shook his head. 'Fine. If getting wet shows you I have a sense of adventure, here I come.'

He squelched out through the muddy grass and knew his shoes would be ruined. His suit jacket and trousers hugged him and his fingers were numb. Standing in front of Ryan, he said, 'You're crazy.'

'Crazy in love,' Ryan said.

'No, just crazy.'

Ryan took Kane's hands again, held them aloft. 'Taste it,' he said, and he stuck his tongue out for the rain. 'It's like an ice cream sundae.'

'It's like copper,' Kane said.

Ryan held his face in his hands, stared deeply into his eyes. 'It tastes like love. It tastes like you. It tastes like Saturday mornings and cold winter nights and hot chocolate and love songs.'

Kane smiled, kissed him, lips already wet moistened more with tongues.

'Can you taste it?' Ryan asked.

'I can,' Kane said, and he really could. He pulled his tie loose, unbuttoned his jacket, turned his face to the thunderous clouds and opened his mouth.

Ryan laughed and twirled on the spot and Kane threw his arms out at right angles from his body, fell backwards to the grass and thought fleetingly of how he'd explain the mud to the dry cleaner. But he pushed that from his mind and thought of nothing but the cold rain stinging his face and actually warming him. He could feel his face already flushed.

Ryan dropped to his side, shoulder to shoulder, and held his hand between their bodies, the grass thick and claggy beneath them. And the world was put to rights. They lay there for twenty minutes, laughing under a canopy of rain needles and talking about nothing of great significance. But to Kane, the words they said that night had more importance than any softly spoken 'I love you' or any model show of affection. The meaningless words they said that night had meaning.

And later that night, at home, they shared a bath and a bottle of wine and warmed their bodies like they warmed their souls.

—

Kane had stretched out on the sofa with a cushion behind his head and another between his arms. He was restless now, needed to be up and doing something but didn't feel like he had the energy to do so. Clark's story of how Ryan came to be a junkie was rolling around in his head like a caged animal. If David was truly behind that first injection, Ryan's first taste of death, Kane vowed he would make him pay.

Officer Burton sat in an armchair, reading a book, and the silence in the flat was penetrating Kane's core, increasing the volume of his thoughts. When Kane's phone vibrated on the coffee table between them, they both looked at it. Burton put his book aside and Kane sat up. They weren't rigged for call monitoring, but when Burton saw the incoming phone number flashing on the screen, he said, 'Must be Clark.'

Kane smiled, picked the phone up and answered it.

'Chinese or Indian?' Clark asked.

'Are you making or buying?' Kane asked, nodding to Burton that his assumption was correct. Burton picked his book up again.

'Please,' Clark scoffed, 'I'm a cop. When would I

have the time to learn how to cook?'

'They don't have cooking classes at cop school?' he asked. 'I'll eat anything right now, I'm starving.'

'Chinese, then,' Clark said. 'I'll be there in an hour.'

Looking at Burton, Kane said, 'Chinese all right with you?'

'You're honoured,' Burton said. 'She only brings Chinese food for the fit lads.'

Kane laughed and Clark said, 'I heard that.'

'Bring a bottle of something nice. I'll pay,' Kane said.

'Getting drunk is never the answer.'

'I said a bottle, not a brewery. You can't deny me a little drink.'

'In that case,' Clark said, 'I'll bring two bottles. How're you holding up?'

'Well, I've stayed in worse accommodation in my time. I think I'll survive.'

'That's the spirit,' Clark said.

They ended the call and Kane stood and stretched his limbs. 'Don't suppose you'd let me out for a jog,' he said, only half joking.

Nodding towards Kane's phone, Burton said, 'You'd be eating my entrails instead of noodles if I did that.'

'She wouldn't be that harsh,' Kane said and he twisted a kink from his neck.

When the front door was forced in without any warning, neither of them had any time to consider their options. Two burly men entered, guns raised, and Burton took a bullet in the face before he could move.

Splashed in Burton's blood, Kane threw himself backwards and flipped over the sofa out of the line of fire, but no more bullets were fired.

The men advanced on him.

Up on his feet, Kane backed away, picked up a footstool and pitched it at them. He quickly backed through the kitchen door and tried to slam it shut but they were right behind him, their guns hanging loosely in their hands.

Reversing through the small kitchen, unwilling to take his eyes off them, Kane pulled a chair out from the table in front of him as though it could act as a barrier. He picked up an empty fruit bowl and threw it at them, an ancient Yellow Pages, the kettle, and kept backing up towards the rear door that serviced a small laundry room that bridged the flat from the world outside.

Nothing unnerved the two men and they came on him with such force that he stumbled against the door and would have fallen to the floor if one of the men hadn't gripped his shirt.

Kane punched him in the stomach, ripped free of his grip, turned.

The other man swung a fist. Kane ducked, punched back, reached for the door handle —

They wrestled him to the ground. One of the men pinned him down and the other, the bigger of the two, raised a foot and brought it down on his chest, kicked him in the side, crouched and punched him square in the face.

Kane spat blood and thrashed wildly with his legs. He clipped one of the men with the side of his foot but the force wasn't enough and they dragged him to his feet, punched him again, and let him fall unconscious between them.

—

When Wilson called her to check in, Clark was less than a few minutes away from the safe house. She let the Bluetooth car stereo pick up the call and

Wilson said, 'When this is all over, I think I'm going to retire.'

'Don't you watch TV?' Clark said. 'The retired cops are always the ones that get caught up in a bank heist or a plot to blow up Parliament.'

'I'll stick to Internet banking and make sure I never have the urge to see Big Ben. I'll see out my days in the garden, drinking homemade cider under the apple tree. Are you on route?'

'I'm taking him dinner. What's the word on our criminal mastermind?'

'Intel hasn't checked in yet. I should be hearing from them any minute. I just got off the phone with Lyon.'

She indicated to turn left, waiting for a gap in the traffic. 'And what do the Frogs want? As if I couldn't guess.'

'They're about to wrap up operations in Spain. They got a hit on the whereabouts of Ramirez and they're just waiting for the nod.'

'How'd they swing that?' Clark asked, pulling off into another street. She drove randomly; years of training meant she often found herself on tail-shaking detours even when she was just driving to the supermarket.

'I daren't ask,' Wilson said. 'But you can guess how hard Lyon's coming down on us right now.'

She turned right, onto the street in which the safe house stood, and said, 'We know where Bernhard is, all we have to do is nab him in the act.'

'Fairy-tale endings and all, right?' Wilson asked.

'A girl can dream,' Clark said. As she drove down the street, she suddenly slammed on the brakes and said, 'Christ!'

'What?'

'Front door's open.' She killed the engine, unfastened her seatbelt.

'Can you see anything?'

She knew Wilson would be on his feet already. She reached into her glove box and withdrew her Taser X26. The intelligent weapon had a range of thirty-five feet and a dataport that recorded device activation. It looked, Clark had commented when they were first issued to the department, like a space-age handgun.

'Where the hell's Burton?' she asked.

'Stay where you are,' Wilson said.

'I'm going to check it out,' she said. 'I'll call you back.'

'Clark, I'm telling you, wait for back up.'

Clark ended the call and stepped out of the car.

As she cautiously approached the house, she held her Taser in both hands, kept close to the wall. 'Police!' she announced as she stood in the open doorway. There was no response. She entered.

Burton was dead in a chair, his face a bloody mess. A footstool that had lost a leg lay upturned in the middle of the room. And Kane was nowhere to be seen.

She scouted the flat and found further evidence of a scuffle in the kitchen, a small amount of blood on the linoleum-covered floor, not enough to indicate that Kane might be dead. Returning to the living room and checking Burton's neck for a pulse, knowing she wouldn't find one, she drew her phone from her pocket and called Wilson back.

'They've got him,' she said. 'They've fucking got him.'

She stood outside until Wilson and the team arrived, sucking fresh air deep into her lungs. She'd seen enough dead bodies over the years for it not to affect her but she could never get used to the smell of spilled blood. PC Burton had been a young man, probably had a wife or a girlfriend.

Maybe even a young kid. She didn't notice if he'd been wearing a wedding ring or not.

He had taken the bullet somewhere in the centre of his face and what was left was thankfully shielded in blood so that she couldn't see the pulp. His shirt, and all the way down to his lap, was stained deep red and the smell of the blood was overpowering.

When the team arrived, along with the coroner, and Burton was wheeled out of the flat on a gurney, Wilson oversaw the operation and then came to Clark.

'I shouldn't have left him,' Clark said.

Wilson pointed at the gurney as they lifted it into the back of the coroner's van. 'And trade places with Burton?'

'Burton was unarmed.'

'And whoever took Kane was armed. You'd have had no chance with a Taser. Don't worry, we'll get him back.'

'Damn right we will,' Clark said.

'I'll call Adams. Get a team together for a briefing. It's time we put a stop to this.'

'Did they follow us to the house?' Clark wondered. 'How else could they find out where he was?'

'We can worry about that later. Right now we need to move and move fast.'

'Bernhard's a step ahead of us. How the hell are we supposed to play this?'

Wilson turned and watched the coroner drive away. 'I have an idea,' he said.

Fifteen

Margaret Bernhard was sitting up in her hospital bed, dark-framed glasses on, flicking through a magazine with her untouched dinner still on the tray in front of her. Since her surgery, she had been recovering well and the memory of Dawson's bullet tearing into her flesh was the dull causality of a distant dream.

She had heard nothing of Kane since he arrived in London and she prayed every night that he was safe, that he was still alive. Whatever feelings she had had for David, though they still throbbed in her chest, were lessening and being replaced by an encompassing anger. She assumed that if Kane had found David there would be only one outcome. She knew Kane would not have taken the derringer like she told him and it was clear that David was a dangerous man. The ones you love, the ones you never suspect, are often the most treacherous.

Twelve years ago, more than a year after the death of her first husband, Ciarán Cassidy, whose surname Ryan still bore, David Bernhard walked into her life and stole her mind as much as he stole her heart. She seldom mixed in financial circles, but she had been invited to a party by a friend and David had enchanted her within five minutes of their introductions. She spoke little to the others present and spent most of the evening on the sofa with him, drinking wine and discussing subjects she would have otherwise considered far too highbrow for her mind. But David had a way with words, a persuasive way of explaining his ideologies to her that she could comprehend his most detailed conversations without breaking a sweat.

By the end of the first hour, they had traded email addresses with promises from David to forward to her some document or other—she no longer remembered what—and by the end of the evening they had exchanged phone numbers and agreed upon a date.

She had worried about Ryan's reaction. Twelve-year-old boys were not generally given to the ready acceptance of their mother's boyfriends.

Boyfriend was more precise; Margaret had not dated anybody since Ciarán's death and finding David had come as an unexpected surprise. Ryan, however, had been fantastic. 'You need someone to keep you busy,' he had said. 'There's only so many times you can tidy my room.'

She had left a friend to watch over Ryan and David had taken her to dinner on their first date. She even remembered what she had ate — asparagus soup, shrimp and rosemary spiedini, pomegranate sorbet. It was things like those that you never forgot.

David enthralled her with his talk of the financial world and the politics that encompassed it. Ciarán had had a highly successful career in sales, and they never went short, but never before had money's prerogative entered her mind. David's witty character had shone that evening and Margaret felt as though she hadn't laughed so much in years, certainly not all through Ciarán's illness and the year that followed his premature death.

David had proposed to her five months later and they were married in a little church in Cork six months after that. Ryan had looked so cute in his

Oxford-grey morning suit, all gangly legs and arms as his growth spurt had become an eruption into early adulthood, his hair soft and combed rather than spiked and hardened by gel. They honeymooned in Switzerland, their hotel room adjoined by Ryan's room who had come along at David's insistence. The pair had hit it off instantly and, although neither believed David to be a replacement for Ryan's dad, they became a close representation of the father-son double act Margaret had seen in years past with Ryan and Ciarán.

Never would she have considered David's ultimate betrayal, that he would be the hand behind the murder of her only son.

Warm thoughts ran cold within her blood.

As she stared at the magazine but saw images of Ryan in her mind, a nurse entered her private room and said, 'You haven't eaten?'

Looking up, Margaret said, 'I'm beginning to feel well again. Are you trying to kill me?' She laughed.

The nurse glanced at the door behind her. 'There are some men here to see you.'

Just then, two men in suits walked in. The one

in front said, 'Thank you, nurse, you can leave now.'

Margaret took her glasses off and adjusted her position on the bed. The nurse hovered nervously before leaving.

'Detectives Simpson and Parker, Mrs Bernhard,' said the first man. They flashed their badges. 'We wonder if you can accompany us to London.' The tone of his voice implied a command, not a request.

'Whatever for?' Margaret asked.

Detective Simpson said, 'We'll explain on the way. We can be in the air within the hour.'

'I'm going nowhere without an explanation.'

Parker wheeled the bed tray away and Simpson said, 'We have instruction from Interpol in London. I'm afraid I can say nothing other than it's in connection with a Mr Kane Rider.'

At the mention of Kane's name, both worried for him as well as relieved that the detectives hadn't come to tell her he was dead, Margaret instantly pulled back the covers, winced at some pain, and slid her legs out of bed. 'Take me home first. I need—'

'There's no time,' Simpson said. 'We have a

helicopter prepping right now.'

'You'll take me home first,' Margaret insisted. 'A lady goes nowhere without her clutch bag.'

Simpson said, 'I must impress upon you the urgency with which we need to act.'

'Impress all you like,' Margaret said. 'You either take me home or I don't get in your damn helicopter.'

Simpson shook his head in dismay and said, 'Come on.'

They helped her out of the bed.

—

Battered in body but not in spirit, unable to see through one black and swollen eye, Kane found a trench within his mind to escape from the nightmare ordeal that his life had become. He settled comfortably into a future-memory — a memory that should have happened but never did, never would.

He had once planned, in a flight of fancy, how he would propose to Ryan.

Always the outgoing one, Ryan was prone to the

necessity of being the focal point of attention. Surrounded by friends, he was a social It Boy, the party animal that everyone loved and admired. Kane, on the other hand, was much more reserved. Certainly no wallflower, but he was the quiet, brooding sort that skirted the boundaries of social engagements, happy to be known as Ryan's Kane, happy to blend into the background while Ryan took the full shine of the spotlight. Where Ryan was chatty and engaging, Kane was soft-spoken and carefully deliberate.

The Union had karaoke on Saturdays and made a change from the Kremlin. Kane, Ryan and a group of Ryan's friends would often visit and have lunch and drinks and sing songs and laugh at how bad they all were. Ryan was up at every chance he could get, finishing one song and selecting his next track almost immediately. He wasn't blessed with the most seductive singing voice in the world, but he could hold a tune.

And every time they went there, Kane was asked to get up and sing—'Do that one you sang me in bed the other night,' Ryan would say—but he always refused; there was a vast difference in singing in the privacy of your own home and belting out love songs on a stage in front of strangers. 'No matter how drunk you get me, you will never get me up in front of this angry mob.'

They egged him and encouraged him, but he would staunchly shake his head and grit his teeth and say no. His social anxiety prevented him from being the centre of attention, from getting up in front of everyone and wilting as they stared at him in gross fascination of whatever song he would butcher.

But he had a plan. One day, enabled by a double helping of Dutch courage, he would speak to the karaoke DJ in advance, tell her his idea, and then, when Ryan and his friends asked him to get up and sing, at first he would refuse, but would suddenly relent and agree, specifying that this would be the one and only time he ever did, saying they'd better film it on their phones if they wanted a keep sake, and he would rise and walk to the front and take the microphone and smile and wait for the music to start.

And just before the first line of the song was to be sung, the DJ would fade out the music and everyone's attention—everyone's—would be on Kane, standing there by the paused lyrics, standing there with a smile on his face and a ring in his pocket. And he would say, 'I know you were expecting me to sing a song, but to be honest I don't have the voice for it.' He wouldn't pause, couldn't pause. 'I'm going to do something a little different,' he'd say. 'There is someone in the room I'd like you all to meet. Ryan, can you stand up?' And Ryan would stand and smile, confused, drink in hand, waving to the captive audience.

'Ryan and I have been going out since we were sixteen,' Kane would continue. 'He's been trying to get me to sing on karaoke since we were first allowed into the bars. Today I said I would, but I won't. Instead, I wondered if no one would mind if I asked him a question.'

Kane would watch Ryan's face for any sign of enlightenment, expecting only uncertainty before he would take the ring box from his pocket and hold it up and say, 'Ryan Cassidy, will you do me the great honour of being my husband?'

And Ryan would scream and the bar's patrons would gasp and applaud when he said yes and there would be much crying and calls for champagne and they would embrace and hold each other tight and fall in love all over again.

Kane already had the memory stored in his head, even though it never happened. At least, he thought, he would always have the memory of wanting to propose to Ryan.

—

The Belgrave Gentleman's Club, situated in the heart of London's Square Mile, was frequented mostly by financial tycoons and wealthy bankers. First established in 1836, it took its name from the district of Belgravia where it was situated until its relocation to the City in 1967. A grand façade gave way to an impressive lobby with two reception rooms at either side of the building and a further eight rooms upstairs, complete with en suite bathrooms, sauna and steam rooms.

At the rear of the Belgrave, a backroom served as an additional meeting place for the more secretive business dealings and offered members a full-sized snooker table, several gambling machines, and a jukebox with discs from Chopin to Led Zeppelin, as well as safe storage and private telephone lines.

David Bernhard was a regular visitor of Belgrave's backroom during his trips to London — membership at the Belgrave was exclusive and member lists were never released to the public.

Currently, he smiled down at Kane, who was on the floor, gagged and bound to a leg of the massive snooker table. The two men who had accosted him from his safe house stood sentry by the door.

David perched on the edge of the table and rolled the cue ball back and forth across the green felt. 'You're a fool, Kane.'

Kane cursed through his gag, his vicious words no more than a mumble. He stared at David with a narrowed eye, the other bruised and closed completely.

'Ryan was like a son to me,' David continued.

The accusation was clear on Kane's face.

'I had no choice. He was in the way.' He rolled the ball into a corner pocket and picked up his gun. A silencer had been screwed to the muzzle.

Kane, resigned to his fate, raised his head with determination. He refused to give David the satisfaction of seeing him cower.

'Don't look at me like that, son,' David said.

Kane stared hard.

David nodded his head. 'How is she?' he asked. 'She did make it, didn't she?'

He had obviously known about Margaret's wound, about the death of Dawson and subsequent events. Kane battled momentarily between confirming the truth and lying. Letting David think Margaret had died in the gunfire back in Belfast may not change anything, but it might dampen David's spirits enough to allow Kane some breathing time. He did love his wife, Kane could see. Although how he could love her and kill her son was beyond Kane's comprehension.

Eventually, reluctantly, Kane nodded.

With a hint of genuine sorrow in his voice, David said, 'Good. I never wanted any of this to happen.'

At the door, David's two goons looked bored, as though abduction and violence were common occurrences, as though David often held a weapon in his hand and had a string of men tied to the snooker table at his feet.

One of the men walked over to the jukebox, pushed a few buttons to select a track, light a cigarette, and returned to his place by the door. From hidden speakers placed around the room,

Janis Joplin's voice scored out her rendition of *Summertime*.

'Twelve years I've loved her,' David said. 'Loved them both.' The gun rested in his hand, a finger placed almost lazily against the trigger. 'You're just like Ryan. If you hadn't interfered, we could have gotten through this. The house, the cars, the clothes—they all have to be paid for. You know nothing.'

He stood, towering over Kane, and then turned, walked across to a mini-bar, put his gun down and poured himself a drink.

'Let's talk,' he said.

One of the men stepped up and removed Kane's gag.

Turning back to face Kane, David said, 'Ryan had something that belonged to me.'

Able to speak at last, Kane moistened his lips and said, 'I don't have it.'

'No,' David said. 'I know you don't. Interpol have it.' He sank the contents of his glass, picked up his gun again and took a solitary step forward. 'Start talking,' he said.

Sixteen

'I don't like it any more than you do,' Wilson said. 'But Rider's right, Bernhard loves her.'

They had handled the officer briefing a little while ago and were now in Wilson's office, suiting up in their ballistic vests. They had already been down to the armoury.

'But using her like this?' Clark asked.

Wilson said, 'It's a last resort. If we get the chance, I want her here for the negotiations.'

'He's not the negotiating type.'

'Which is why we have the ace,' Wilson said.

Clark sighed. She hated wearing the vest but had already felt, first hand, the protection it offered. It had been a particularly violent raid on a trafficking operation in Manchester six years ago.

Lyon had been tracking the organisation for a while before they were able to mount busts in both the UK and Libya, a country where the forced labour and sexual exploitation of illegal migrants was endemic, as well as their exportation to other countries.

Wilson had headed up the UK task force and Clark had only been a detective for two years. She was a subordinate and always knew her place, carried out orders to the letter, and filed comprehensive reports that shamed many others on the team with their detail and detachment. But on this particular raid, she let her heart cloud her mind and acted impulsively. They had every reason to suspect that the property they were raiding contained not just the traffickers but also a number of forced Asian prostitutes, women who had been too afraid to go to the police or make a run for it—those who tried to run where usually caught and butchered in the most horrendous ways.

Clark had given it too much thought, allowed her feelings to get in the way of the operation, a straightforward enter-and-extract situation.

Dawn raids were mostly successful because they held the element of surprise. They had taken down both the front and rear entrances simultaneously. In Libya, their counterparts were acting in unison.

The UK team stormed the building and were almost immediately under fire. Wilson issued orders for cover and consideration, but Clark had seen a young girl, no more than fifteen, running naked through a door to her right. 'Got a vic,' she shouted, referring to the girl as a victim, and she took off after her.

She followed the girl into the room, weapon raised, ready in case any of the perpetrators were in there, and discovered the girl alone, on her knees beside a makeshift and messy bed, rummaging in a hessian sack.

Clark lowered her gun. 'It's okay,' she said. 'We're going to get you out of here.' The Asian girl looked up at her, eyes wild with fear, and Clark asked, 'Where are the men?'

The girl said something in her native tongue, lost in translation, and pulled her hand from the sack. Before Clark knew it, the girl was shooting at her. The bullet hit her squarely in the chest. When Clark went down, stunned but not unconscious, she saw, foggily, Wilson standing over her and firing at the girl. Her blood coated her naked body like a sheet.

Wilson checked Clark's vest for impact, took her

hand, helped her stand, and said, 'Everyone's allowed one mistake. Next time I give you an order, if you ignore it, I'll shoot you myself.'

When the operation was locked down and marked up as a success, Clark was treated for a cracked rib and Wilson said, 'Come on, you owe me a drink for that.' They had been firm colleagues—even friends—after that.

Now, she secured her vest and said, 'It's not often we get to play the tough guys any more.'

'Enjoy it while it lasts,' Wilson said.

'I'll be glad when it's over. I'm getting too old for the theatrics.'

Wilson laughed. 'You'll never be too old for a showdown.'

Outside the office door, Dixon slouched by. Life on the top floor with Biggs was clearly getting to him. 'Dixon,' Wilson called.

Dixon stopped, smiled. 'Yes, boss?'

'Don't call me that. And suit up. We need all the men we can get.'

'Is Adams on board?'

'We have our man cornered,' Wilson said. 'We'll tell Adams later that we pulled you off your important paperwork.'

'Yes, boss,' Dixon said. He hurried down the corridor.

'Are we sure,' Clark asked, 'that they have him at the Belgrave?'

'They were seen going in through the back entrance. Couldn't be sure it was Rider but if it wasn't, Bernhard's playing two games.'

'How'd they get passed Intel?' Clark asked.

'Watch me get my hands on Mickey Brown.'

'Mickey Brown's a tank. I'd pay to see that.'

Checking each other's straps, Wilson said, 'You gamble too much.'

'Only on sure-fire wins.'

Wilson lifted his gun from the desk and checked the magazine. 'Good to go?'

'Let the fun commence,' Clark said.

—

David slapped the butt end of a cue across Kane's face and Kane spat the resulting blood on the carpeted floor, his cheek stinging and his head hollow.

'I told you before, I don't know anything.'

With his arms behind his back, still tied to the leg of the snooker table, his whole body had gone numb. And he was sure he had heard something snap inside his face two cue-slaps ago. His chin and his shirt were berry-red with blood.

'Don't lie to me,' David said, poking the cue into Kane's chest with every word.

'They're hardly going to tell me anything, are they? I'm not the police.'

'You got close to them.'

David had been pressing him for as much information as he could gain about Ryan's involvement with Interpol and how much they knew.

'Ryan got close to them,' Kane said. 'I knew nothing.'

'The correspondence Ryan gave them — do you know what it contained?'

'Correspondence?' Kane said. He laughed.

David knocked the cue off Kane's right temple again.

'That's what this is about?' Kane asked. 'Correspondence? Love letters between you and your arms dealers?' He laughed again.

David raised the cue again and when Kane

refused to flinch, he lowered it. 'I don't want to hurt you, Kane.'

Kane stared, defiant. 'I'd love to hurt you.'

'You give me no choice,' David said. 'I never wanted any of this to happen.'

Kane shook his head, more blood splashing the carpet, and he winced. 'Go to hell,' he said. 'I'm so glad you're not his real dad. Ryan was a bigger man than you'll ever be, you fat ugly fuck.'

He was taunting him, almost begging David to hit him again. More than anything, he wanted this to be over. One way or another, it was going to end. And right now, he saw only one way out. When the end came, it would be welcomed, it would be embraced. And maybe Ryan—sweet, lovely Ryan—would be there to meet him. How could he have gotten it so wrong? The doubt that crept in after Ryan's death was a curse that was finally broken.

'You think it's so simple, don't you?' David said. 'If only you knew the sacrifices I've made.'

'You call killing Ryan a sacrifice?'

'I did what I had to.'

'By murdering him?'

David shook his head. 'It wasn't like that.' He

turned, sat the cue on the snooker table and picked up his gun. He pointed it at Kane's face. 'All I ever wanted was the best for my family.'

'Do you have any idea how fucked up that sounds?' Kane asked.

David's mobile phone started ringing, but he ignored it. 'The last thing you want to do now is piss me off, Kane.'

'That's exactly what I'm trying to do.'

The phone kept ringing.

'I like you, son. You've got balls, that's for sure.'

'You want to see them?' Kane goaded. If he was going out, he was going out in style.

David turned away in disgust, finally answered his phone. 'What?'

On the other end of the line, Detective Dixon said, 'You better hope you're not in the Belgrave in five minutes.'

'Where are you now?' David asked.

'I'm heading to a backup van. I can't hold them off,' Dixon said. 'They're already on their way — three vans, four cars and a big fucking brass band.'

David terminated the call.

'Jesus,' he said to Kane. 'Are you having fun, yet? Because it's about to get a whole lot more interesting.' To his goons, he said, 'Pick him up.'

He sat his gun back down and walked over to the rank of safes on the far wall. Punching in a security code on the panel, he unlocked a safe and withdrew a hard-shell suitcase, handling it with extreme care.

As his men untied Kane and dragged him to his feet, David placed the suitcase on the clean, green felt of the snooker table, sweat glistening on his upper lip and forehead.

He twisted the combination locks and slowly eased the lid open.

Seventeen

When they arrived outside the Belgrave club, Wilson issued immediate orders for a fan-formation around the front and rear of the building while the Met police officers were on crowd dispersal duties.

Once his officers were in place, Wilson and Clark ran in a crouch towards Mickey Brown, head of Intelligence. The sun was down behind the buildings to their left and night was dragging shadows behind it.

'Give,' Wilson said to Brown.

Mickey Brown, six foot three inches of vicious bulldog, had been in Intelligence since his late twenties and had worked closely with Wilson's team on many occasions.

'Thermal imaging shows us four bodies,' he said. 'All in the same room. We're trying to get a directional mic rigged up but it's going to be from across the street. We can't get near.'

'How soon?'

'Five minutes, tops.'

'What's the scene?' Wilson asked. The police officers were stretching tape across either end of the street.

Brown pointed. 'We have guns on rooftops, there, there and there. Exits are covered and we've got more men in the vicinity if they get round us.'

'They won't,' Wilson said.

He hooked an earpiece over his right ear and thumbed a dial on his radio.

Brown said, 'They say you're bringing in the birdie.'

Wilson nodded. 'She's on her way. PSNI picked her up earlier.'

'I don't like you bringing civilians to my party, Wilson.'

Clark scanned the surrounding area. 'None of us like it.'

'I'm hoping we won't need her,' Wilson said. 'But if Bernhard won't talk to us, he'll talk to her.'

'You better be damn sure about that,' Brown said.

—

A police helicopter landed on a helipad at London's City Airport and the door slid back as WPC Scoles ran towards it, pushing a wheelchair.

Detectives Simpson and Parker jumped out of the helicopter and Parker turned back to help Margaret out. They eased her gently into the wheelchair and started back towards the terminal building.

Margaret kept her eyes straight ahead, gripping her clutch bag protectively. The two detectives had tried to argue with her, but Margaret was a woman not to be trifled with; they detoured by her house and allowed her to pack a change of clothes and bring a few personal effects, on the proviso that she be no more than two minutes in the house.

Upstairs, alone in her room as she quickly threw leggings and a sweatshirt into an overnight bag, she had double-checked the detectives were still downstairs and she took her derringer from the nightstand. She had dropped it into her handbag and clasped it shut. Downstairs, as they ushered her out of the house and back into their car, she made a show of opening the small leather clutch bag and pulling out a tissue, in the hope that they'd assume if she had something to hide she wouldn't have been so forthright.

There had been no metal detectors, no scanners, when they whisked her through airport security in Belfast and helped her to board the helicopter.

Now, holding the bag safely in her lap as they wheeled her into the terminal, Scoles said, 'They're already at the scene. We have a van waiting outside.'

Detective Simpson said, 'Is anyone willing to tell us what's going on?'

'You know as much as I do,' said Scoles. 'It's Interpol,' she added, by way of explanation.

'Secrets and hierarchy,' Simpson said. 'Just another day at the office.'

Scoles ran through what little she did know, that Bernhard was holed up in a building, had a hostage—likely Kane Rider—and that Interpol were gunning for it. Margaret's involvement was nothing more than conjecture.

In the police van, the driver flipped on his blues and they went at speed through the streets of London.

Simpson made a call and clarified a few pertinent issues and when he hung up he faced Margaret.

'This is as much as we know,' he said. 'We believe Mr Rider is with your husband and Interpol need to get him out. They have the building surrounded and they have a hostage negotiation team on hand. They're hoping to end this fairly easily, but if they need you to talk some sense into your husband, they'll ask for your help. You won't be placed in any danger and until they require you, you'll be kept back at a safe distance. Do you understand?'

Margaret closed her eyes and nodded. Her face was ashen.

The driver's radio squawked and the dispatcher's tinny voice said, 'Delta Seven, confirm location.'

'This is Seven,' the driver said. 'Currently pulling off St Thomas Street, ETA three minutes.'

Eyes still closed, Margaret breathed through her nose and tried to relax her shoulders. Perturbed by her stillness, Simpson said, 'Mrs Bernhard? You're looking a little pale. Are you all right?'

She didn't answer him.

'Are you going to pass out, Mrs Bernhard?'

Margaret opened her eyes, hugged her bag for security, and said, 'I'll be fine.'

—

Eyes closed, she swayed with the movement of the police van and allowed her mind to remember peaceful times — Ryan on his sixth birthday, clomping up and down the garden wearing only his swimming trunks, a pair of her high heels and a string of beads around his neck; Ciarán reading bedtime stories to their son about dragons and wizards and mischievous elves who'd sooner steal your shoes than mend them; Ryan at five, waving at her from a merry-go-round as she prayed he wouldn't fall off and called for him to hold on tight.

Margaret and Ryan had always been very close, brought closer still by the loss of his father during his formative years. Ryan's confusion was more about his father's illness than his own sexuality. He had never formally come out; it was something that Margaret had always seemed to know, something accepted as truth without spoken word, like a devout Catholic's belief in Christ.

He had once tried to say the words. By that point, she had known for many years, though he was never exactly camp or effeminate. Perhaps not all mothers know these things, but the close bond they had shared awarded her with an insight of uncommon clarity.

They had moved into David's new-build home and Ryan had started his GCSE year at school, where he had met and quickly fallen in love with Kane. She had never suspected for one minute that the sixteen-year-old equivalent of true love would have been the real thing. Not many people find real love so early in life, although she had been seventeen when she met Ciarán.

She had met Kane a handful of times in those first few months, watched from the pedestal that Ryan had placed her on as the two boys' friendship grew and developed. He had stayed for dinner and she had seen the smiles and hooded exchanges between them.

When Ryan had come to her one evening as she prepared their evening meal, always enough in the pot for Kane in case he decided to stay long enough to eat, David tapping violently on his computer keyboard in his office above them, Ryan had ventured, 'Mum?'

'Wash your hands,' Margaret had said. 'Grab me some basil, will you, please?'

Ryan had complied, standing shoulder to shoulder with her as he watched her chopping the green leaves. He remained silent throughout.

Scraping the basil from the chopping board into the pan, Margaret said, 'What's on your mind, darling?'

He shrugged his shoulders.

'Is Kane staying?' Kane had come over with Ryan straight from school and they had been playing video games in his room all evening.

'That's the thing,' Ryan said. He offered no more.

Checking on the oven, Margaret said, 'His Mum'll think we've kidnapped him soon enough. We should have her over.'

'Can Kane...' Ryan tried.

'Can Kane what?'

'Do you mind if he stays over?'

She frowned at the oven and turned the temperature down. 'Of course not, honey. If his mother's all right with it.'

'Cool,' Ryan said. But he didn't leave her side.

'It'll be ready in ten minutes,' Margaret said.

'Mum?'

'Yes?'

'What I mean is,' Ryan said, and paused momentarily. 'Can he stay over in my room?'

The words were heavily laden and dripping. Margaret wiped her hands on a tea towel, neatly folded it before she answered him. 'Yes, love.'

She watched Ryan chew on his upper lip. 'You know what that means, don't you?' he asked.

She held his shoulders, smiled at him, kissed his forehead. 'Yes, love. I know what that means. You'll be careful, won't you?'

He nodded, his face full of relief and excitement. When he left the kitchen she turned back to the pot on the stove. She closed her eyes and laughed giddily.

'It means I don't have to make up a spare room,' she said to herself.

And as the police van rocked and sped through the streets of London, as she was pushed towards a destiny she could not imagine, she clung to that heart-to-heart conversation with her only son, and realised that life was all subtext. People refrain from saying what they really mean. What is not said is far more important than what is spoken.

—

When Margaret's police van swung into view at the end of the street, behind the police cordon, Wilson keyed his radio. He, Clark, Dixon and the others had spread out around the front of the building, crouched and protected behind parked cars.

'She's here,' he said. 'We need to keep her behind the tape for now.'

Clark, two car lengths along the street, nodded and said to her radio, 'Dixon, get on it.'

'Yes, ma'am,' came his professional reply. He ran down the street to the tape line as Detective Simpson wheeled Margaret down the van's ramp.

Simpson fitted a small earpiece to Margaret's ear and said, 'The trained negotiator is going to be on the end of this. He'll give you constant direction on what to say and how to say it, if and when they need you, okay?'

Just then, the front door of the Belgrave

Gentleman's Club swung open.

Everyone tensed, their weapons trained on the dark entrance.

A figure stepped out. Slowly.

Uttering a curse, Wilson saw that it was Kane. He was naked to the waist and strapped to his chest was an explosive device. A release cable ran from the base of the bomb to an ignition switch in his hand. Kane's thumb was already pressed down on the button.

He was sweaty and bloody and shaking, one eye bruised and closed, his other darting around, panic clearly visible on his face. 'Don't shoot,' he said, his voice broken. He raised his arms in supplication, his thumb still on the button.

'Jesus,' Wilson said. To his radio, he said, 'get a BD team down here fast.'

He adopted a firing stance, his gun trained on Kane.

'Kane? What's going on, mate?'

Down the street, Margaret was straining in her wheelchair to see what was happening. She was too far away and there were too many obstacles in her way to allow her a clear vision of the club.

'What's happening? I can't see.'

Dixon stepped up beside Simpson and said, 'It's all right, I've got her from here.'

'She's under my protection detail,' Simpson said.

'Someone tell me what's going on,' Margaret said.

Dixon took the handles of Margaret's wheelchair and said to Simpson, 'You're relieved of your duties, Officer.'

'It's Detective,' Simpson said. 'And you have no authority.'

'Man,' Dixon laughed, 'I'm Interpol. I have authority over everything. Step aside.'

Along the street, Wilson was saying, 'Come on, Kane. Talk to me. What's the deal?'

Kane said, 'I can't. Let go. Explode.'

Margaret said, 'I can't see what's going on. Where's Kane? Where's David. Get me up there.'

Dixon put a staying hand on her shoulder. 'We're just going to sit here and watch the show for now, love.' He wheeled Margaret away from the others and he leaned in close, whispering, 'Listen, sweetheart. That husband of yours—we sort of have a little understanding. I want you to tell him something for me, okay?'

Eighteen

From behind her cover, Ann Clark aimed her gun, sighting it between Kane and the club's door. Bernhard still had to be inside.

Trained for intense situations, she quickly took in the scene without losing her focus. The club was surrounded, front and back. Snipers were stationed on rooftops and the police had cordoned off the street and ensured neighbouring buildings were evacuated. A crowd had gathered at either end of the road, intent on viewing whatever spectacle there was to be seen.

To one side, Dixon had taken on babysitting duties of Margaret Bernhard, and Clark was grateful that, from Margaret's position, she could see very little. She had only ever seen Ryan's mother in photographs before now. She had known her to be a strong-willed woman with an independent mind.

NCIS had ruled Mrs Bernhard out of their inquiry almost a year ago, months before Ryan ever came forward as a witness and potential asset. They had been following Bernhard and his associates for some time. He had long favoured himself as the family man and often brought Margaret along to his meetings, speaking in code and displaying her like a prize while ensuring she knew nothing of the true nature of his business affairs.

Interpol's Northern Ireland team assigned to the operations reported on Margaret's whereabouts for months before they marked her as non-threatening. They were told by London to maintain observations throughout but to assume a relaxed view of her involvement. It was recent events, particularly the murder of her son, that pointed to her innocence and ultimately led to Pat Wilson's decision to bring her over now.

Clark still wasn't sure about the idea—using a civilian for negotiations went against everything she had been taught, everything she had learned—but Wilson was her superior and she bowed to his better judgement.

With her peripheral vision alert to change, she

kept her gun raised and stared at Kane and the doorway behind him.

Kane was clearly panicked, his body tense, and he was using all his concentration on keeping the detonator in his hand depressed.

She watched as he kept his hands in the air, his arms wavering slightly, and she saw tears on his cheeks. Whatever Bernhard had used to beat Kane's face with, he had done a good job.

Wilson said, 'It's all right, Kane. I know you're not going to let go of the release.'

'What do I do?' Kane begged.

'Keep your finger down. You can do it. We'll get you out of it in a minute. Where's—?'

David Bernhard loomed in the doorway, breaking shadows and hovering on the threshold. His greying hair was dishevelled and sweat beaded his face. He raised a gun and pointed it at the back of Kane's head.

'I'm here,' he said. 'Anyone moves, I put a hole in the back of his skull and we all go up.'

Clark tightened her grip on her handgun and kept a steady aim.

Wilson took one sideways step, closer to the front of the car he had been tucked behind. 'All you'll succeed in doing is blowing him and yourself up, Bernhard. Where's the fun in that?' He had seen similar explosives used in the past and the blast radius was confined.

David laughed, cold and harsh. 'Not with three pounds of ball bearings encased in the C4,' he said. 'You know the kind of damage that can do?'

Clark cursed, quickly clocked up the number of people around her, most of them secreted behind vehicles. It really wasn't looking like a good idea to have Margaret Bernhard in the middle of it all and she could see from Mickey Brown's face that he felt the same way.

Wilson's radio burst to life and a sniper said, 'I have the shot.'

Wilson raised a hand. 'Hold off. Let's talk this over, David.'

'You gonna boil the kettle?' David asked. 'I could murder a brew.'

'Mate,' Wilson said, 'if you want to come and talk, I'll make you a cup of tea myself.'

'I have nothing to say to you,' David said.

Wilson took another step. 'I didn't think you would.'

'Stay where you are,' David shouted.

Into her radio, Clark said, 'Easy, Pat. Now's not the time.'

Wilson ignored her, signalled down the street to Dixon. 'I have someone you might want to talk to. Dixon, bring her up. Not too close.'

Dixon raised the police tape and wheeled Margaret inside the barrier. 'Remember what I said,' he told her, his voice low. 'Tell him to keep his mouth shut or it's going to be bad for everyone.'

Margaret settled her clutch bag in her lap, allowed Dixon to wheel her forward and, barely moving her lips, said, 'Fuck off.'

—

He had no idea what to do. When David had carefully strapped the bomb to his chest, Kane hadn't expected this. What he had expected, what he had hoped for, was that David would set a timer, leave Kane in the building, and flee the scene. But now, with his thumb on a detonator and the risk of killing other people, innocent people, Kane was beyond terrified.

A few minutes ago, inside the club, he had hoped for an end. He had nothing left to live for — Ryan had been his life for eight years and despite the doubt, despite the recent revelations, he knew that he could never love anybody else. When the government put its backing behind civil partnerships, they had even discussed the possibility of getting married, of making it official. Before all this, Kane would have been willing to give up his life for Ryan. Because of all this, he was willing to give up his life to be with him.

When he saw Margaret being wheeled forward, he sobbed. 'Margaret,' he cried.

Behind him, David said, 'Jesus, what is this? *This is Your Life?*'

'Let's put the guns down and chat, eh?' Wilson said.

'Hi, honey,' David said. 'I would have called but...I've sort of had my hands full here.'

Kane kept his eyes on Margaret, kept his shoulders taut, kept his thumb on the detonator.

Standing behind Margaret, Dixon put a firm hand on her shoulder.

'Dixon,' David said, smiling.

'Tell him,' Dixon whispered to Margaret.

'I thought I smelt your disease,' David continued. 'Had any more kids since I paid off the last whore for you? Get your grubby hands off my wife.'

Wilson and Clark snapped their heads round to Dixon but Wilson just as quickly trained his gun back on David. Clark aimed firmly at Dixon.

'Dixon?' she questioned.

'What? The man's a lunatic.'

Clark nodded to Detectives Simpson and Parker. 'I knew you were a weasel,' she said, 'but a rat?'

Simpson and Parker were on him instantly, restraining him, removing his weapon and radio, and they cuffed him.

David laughed. 'Never trust a copper. They're all bent,' he said.

Wilson said, 'I'll deal with you later, Dixon. Mrs Bernhard, are you all right?'

Dixon protested his innocence but Clark said, 'Save it for the inquest.'

Margaret nodded, said, 'Get me closer.'

'Stay where you are, love,' David called to her.

'Don't call me love.'

'What do you say we go on a holiday when this is over, eh? Just you and me.'

'Somebody take me closer,' Margaret said. 'He'll listen to me. I can make him see sense.' She looked directly at Wilson. 'Trust me. I know him better than anybody.'

An officer stepped up behind Margaret and looked to Wilson for clarification. Wilson nodded, said, 'Not too close.'

'Stay where you are,' David said again.

Kane took a deep breath, said, 'No,' and pressed his lips together.

'Come on, David, let's not be foolish here,' Wilson said.

—

'I'll blow his head off, I swear I will.' David stepped out of the gloomy doorway and pressed his gun to Kane's head. 'Margaret?' he said, half questioning, half commanding.

Margaret gripped the small bag in her lap and from her earpiece, the negotiator said, 'Keep your voice calm, love. I'm with you. Tell him you're here to help him sort this out.'

'What the hell are you playing at, David?' she

said.

'Cool it,' the negotiator advised her. 'Tell him it's all right, there is a way out.'

'I did this for us,' David said. She could see the anger and the strain on his face.

She took a deep breath. 'You killed my son.' Saying it aloud, finally acknowledging the fact, created a pain in her chest. She knew it was a psychological pain rather than a physical one, but it hurt nonetheless.

'It was an accident,' David said.

'He was stabbed,' Margaret told him. 'What kind of an accident is that?'

'We were in Spain,' David said. 'They were only supposed to rough him up, not kill him. Margaret, please.' She detected a slight crack in his voice. 'You have to believe me. I could never do something to hurt you.'

From his position by a parked car, Wilson took another step.

'Stay where you are,' David said. 'I mean it.'

'He was my son,' Margaret told him.

'I love you,' David said.

'Don't you dare say that. You love no one but yourself, you selfish, pig-headed, evil bastard.'

—

Kane felt the gun against the back of his head, felt the rivulets of sweat on his back. Margaret was uncomfortably close if the bomb on his chest was going to go off and he was convinced he couldn't keep his finger on the detonator for much longer. He could already feel the nerves twitching in his hand, feel the muscles cramping.

Sweat and fear stung his eyes and his legs were weak.

When David had said he loved Margaret and she retaliated with obscenities, Kane felt the pressure of the gun on his head slacken, knew that David was turning to face his wife.

'How can you say that?' David asked. 'You know I love you.'

Impulse brought life to Kane's limbs. Sensing David's attention shifting, he turned, grabbed David's arm, swung himself around and pulled David in tight to him, David's back against Kane's chest, against the bomb.

David brought the gun up, the cold muzzle hard against Kane's jaw.

'Go on, shoot me, you bastard,' Kane said. 'Blow yourself up.'

'You want to take everyone else down with us?'

David's body was twisted, his arm across his chest as he pressed the gun firmly into Kane's flesh.

'Not with you shielding the explosion,' Kane said.

David said, 'Those ball bearings will rip right through me and still take everyone else out.'

Wilson took another step, kept his gun aimed and ready. 'Let him go, Kane. You don't want to do this.'

'He killed Ryan,' Kane said to Margaret.

Clark said, 'Kane.'

'I know, love,' Margaret said. 'But let him go.'

'He killed him.'

'It's all right, Kane. Let him go.' Margaret rocked once in her chair as though the motion would propel her forward.

'No,' Kane said.

'Go on,' David growled. 'Be a good little boy. Do as you're told, son.'

'I'm not your fucking son.'

Margaret raised an arm, her hand upturned,

beseeching. 'Let him go.'

'I'll kill him,' Kane said.

Another step from Wilson. 'Don't do it, Kane. We'll end this a better way.'

Kane wavered, felt the anger leave him like the tide of a burst dam. He loosened his grip on David but didn't want to let go. There was no other way, why couldn't they see that?

David pulled away from him and turned. He grabbed Kane's hair, yanked his head back and jammed the gun up under his ear. The force twisted Kane's head further.

'Bad move…son,' David said.

'Easy now,' Wilson cautioned. Clark had stepped out from behind her cover and Kane felt like every gun in the world was pointed straight at him.

'You see what we have to deal with, honey?' David said. He nodded at the multitude of officers. He jerked Kane's head further still. 'All this is his fault. If it wasn't for him, you and I could be away somewhere.'

'Leave Kane alone,' Margaret said. 'This is between us now. Let him go.'

David took a step towards her, dragging Kane

with him.

With the pressure on his body and the sweat in his hands, he was sure his thumb would slip and the bomb would explode.

'I loved you and look what happens,' David said.

—

Margaret quickly realised that changing the way she spoke to him might affect how he reacted. In her ear, the negotiator had told her she needed to calm him down, needed to get him to see sense. At the very least, they needed Kane removed and dealt with by the bomb disposal team. With the threat of the bomb eliminated, they could do more to stop David.

The negotiator said, 'Whatever it takes, we need to keep him cool.'

She could forgive herself later. 'You love me,' she said, smiling. 'That's all that matters.'

'But love isn't going to fix this,' David said. He twisted harder on Kane's head. 'Love isn't going to help any more.'

She felt like a fraud. 'We can make it work.'

'You love me, too?' David asked.

'Of course I do.'

'We can go away somewhere.'

'We can talk about it,' she told him.

David took another step towards her, removed the gun from Kane's neck and flicked it in the direction of Wilson and Clark. 'But they won't let me.'

'You got yourself in some trouble,' she said. 'That's all. We'll get through it.'

'How?' David asked.

'We always do, don't we? We'll find a way. Let Kane go. Everything's going to be just fine.'

'No,' David said. 'As soon as I let him go, they'll shoot me.' The look on his face was one of impudence mixed with childish fear.

'I won't let them,' Margaret said.

David stared at her, his eyes glassy. For a long moment, she thought he might kill Kane anyway. She smiled at him, forced her face to remain calm and her lips turned.

'I won't let them,' she repeated.

What went through his mind at that moment, she had no idea. Perhaps he had been so affected by his actions that his brain no longer worked the way it should. She was convinced her words would not have been enough to make him turn himself in.

He released his hold on Kane, but kept his gun raised at his face. Kane took a step backwards, his thumb still on the detonator.

'Come here, honey,' Margaret said, one arm raised for an embrace.

David moved slowly towards her, his head flicking between her and Kane.

'It's okay,' Margaret said. 'We'll get through this, you know we will.'

David smiled at her and for an instant, for just the briefest moment, she saw the old David, the man she fell in love with all those years ago, before the image was replaced by the vision—the revulsion—of Ryan's body in a coffin.

She kept her arm outstretched. She saw him worrying at his lower lip with his teeth, the way he used to do when he struggled with a Sudoku at the breakfast table. And then he lowered his gun, leaned into her embrace, and held her tight.

—

Instantly, Wilson, Clark, Brown and the rest of the officers swooped in to secure the situation. More officers stormed inside the building.

Mickey brown took Kane by the arm. 'Easy now. This way.'

Kane heard Wilson say, 'Drop the gun, Bernhard.'

Brown tried to lead him away from the scene but Kane refused. 'Not until Margaret's safe,' he said.

'She's fine,' Brown said. 'There's no time. We need to get that off you fast.'

David clung to Margaret as Wilson and Clark slowly approached, their guns aimed and ready to fire, just in case.

'Drop it,' Wilson said.

David looked up, pointed his gun at Wilson. 'Back off, I mean it.'

With Brown's hand covering Kane's thumb on the detonator, acting as extra pressure in case Kane's muscles gave out, Kane saw Margaret reach out and touch David's cheek.

'It's okay, it's okay,' she soothed.

David kept his gun pointed at Wilson and he nuzzled Margaret's neck. 'I did it all for you,' he

said.

Kane pulled free of Brown's grip, stepped forward. 'Get away from her, you bastard. I swear I'll blow us all up.'

Clark swung round. 'Stand down, Kane.'

'I'll do it.'

'It's in hand,' she said.

David twisted, wrapped an arm around Margaret's neck and pointed the gun at her head. 'Back off. All of you just back off.'

Margaret was expressionless.

'Give it up, Bernhard,' Wilson said. 'Don't do this.'

'Let her go or I'll blow us up.'

'I'll kill her first,' David said.

Kane raised the release cable in front of him. 'I'm going to let go.'

'Don't be so foolish, Kane,' Wilson said.

Kane kept his eyes on Margaret. How could this have happened? What laws of chaos could allow for Margaret's own husband to hold a gun to her head?

Perhaps unnoticed by everyone else, Kane saw Margaret slip a hand inside her clutch bag.

'Just back off,' David said again.

She pulled her hand back out and she was holding something.

'Drop your weapon, Bernhard,' Wilson said. 'There's no way out.'

Brown took Kane's arm again, stared at the scene in front of them. He stepped in front of Kane. 'She has a gun!'

Her face still stony and unreadable, Margaret aimed upwards and fired off a round.

Blood rained on her head and her lap. David jolted, wobbled. He fell face down in her knees and his body twitched. The bullet had taken his chin and exploded from the back of his head.

Wilson and Clark shifted their aim to Margaret, but she dropped the derringer and slowly raised her hands above her head.

Kane lurched forward, attempted to go to Margaret, but Brown kept a tight grip on his arm. 'Margaret!' he shouted.

'Easy,' Brown said. 'Keep your finger on that button.'

When Margaret spoke, her voice was as calm and dead as her face. 'Get him off me,' she said.

Clark moved in, pushed David's body to the ground and checked his pulse. She holstered her gun as Wilson looked around and surveyed the scene.

Some officers exited the Belgrave Gentleman's Club with two burly goons. The rest of the building, they reported, was clear. Bernhard was dead—and they were going to have one hell of a report to file.

As bomb disposal officers surrounded Kane, he felt hot tears on his cheeks but hadn't realised he'd been crying. When the men eased his thumb from the detonator and replaced it in one movement with thick black tape, Kane's hand cramped and twitched. His legs gave way and they caught him before he fell. 'You're okay,' one of the guys said. 'Let's get this thing off you, eh?'

Relieved of the burden, Kane finally dropped to his knees and sobbed.

Nineteen

Belfast in September was dull but the air was calm and the sun still had some life in it. Wispy clouds scudded across the expanse above and the trees that bordered the western slope of the cemetery were tall and majestic sentinels.

The gentle breeze brought with it the smell of autumn and the pledge of an early frost. The winter would be a harsh one but for now summer was reluctant to give way.

Kane had overseen the installation of Ryan's headstone only yesterday, the temporary wooden cross removed and the marble marker laid in its place. Today, walking between the neat rows of graves and carrying a large bouquet of flowers, he wondered about the future, a future without Ryan, a future without love. Last month's events in London had taken their toll and haunted his dreams like they haunted his waking moments.

Fearful of vendetta by David Bernhard's associates, Interpol had placed him in the care of guards who watched him around the clock. Even now they stalked the perimeter of the cemetery. He felt like this was no longer his own life, as though he no longer had purpose and meaning. But he would learn to cope on his own.

He approached Ryan's graveside and looked down at the marker. Inlaid above Ryan's name was a photograph of him, a head-and-shoulder shot taken last year. Below that the words, Cherished son and soul mate. Forever in our hearts.

Kane drew his upper lip into his mouth and breathed deeply through his nose, inhaling the sweet scent of the flowers.

When Pat Wilson cleared his throat behind him, he turned and smiled. He and Ann Clark had come over from London a few days ago. They sat with him then and discussed his future, his options. Seeing them again brought the nightmare back to life.

What they had talked to him about when they first arrived had sent his head into a spin. The things they said, the offer they made, both repulsed and moved him in equal measure.

The Spanish team's luck had run out and their target, Ramirez, had managed to get away. He had gone underground, they told Kane, and it looked as though operations were stepping up again. Lyon wasn't happy with the outcome of the London debacle and the failure of those in Spain only added to their fury. The pressure was on to stem the war and protect the innocent — and Kane was a likely target.

'How're you holding up?' Wilson asked.

Kane shrugged. 'I've been better.'

'It'll take some time to get used to,' Clark said, 'but you'll be fine.'

He nodded. 'How's the case going?' he asked.

Clark touched Kane's arm. 'Like we said the other day, operations have collapsed in Spain, but we're still making headway in France and the Ukraine. Jim Dixon was tried last week.'

'I'm sure he loves it in Wandsworth,' Wilson said. 'Bent copper behind bars; they'll be having a field day.'

'Did he confess?' Kane asked.

'Still protesting his innocence,' Clark said. 'But his house and his computer were searched and they found enough evidence to put him away for a long time.'

Kane nodded again. 'She's still coming, isn't she?'

Wilson checked his watch. 'Should be here any minute. I told you, we have friends where it counts.'

'I can't believe,' Kane said, 'that this is how it ends.'

'You can change your mind if you want,' Wilson said.

Kane flatted his lips. 'No.'

When a police van drove into the cemetery and stopped a short distance from where they stood, Kane felt his chest constrict. Margaret was taken from a ramp at the back of the van, still in a wheelchair, and she looked tiny and feeble. She had been taken into custody after shooting David and transferred back to Belfast three days later. The date for her trial had not yet been set and being in remand was clearly doing her no favours. She had promised him that she was being treated well and assured him her solicitor said she had a good case.

A police officer wheeled her along the path and set the brakes. He nodded at Wilson and Clark and stepped aside, allowing them some privacy. Interpol had pulled some strings to have her here today and the PSNI were under strict instructions to comply.

Margaret took Kane's hand in one of hers, Clark's in the other. To Wilson, she said, 'Thank you.'

Wilson smiled.

'Are you okay?' Kane asked.

She squeezed his hand and looked down at Ryan's headstone. 'He's at peace now.' Her smiled was delicate.

As a cool breeze stirred around them, Kane removed his jacket and draped it over Margaret and she pulled it around her shoulders. He looked at Wilson, Clark.

Wilson nodded. Clark smiled.

He turned back to the grave and looked down. 'Happy birthday, Ryan.' He crouched, touched the headstone, and placed the bouquet of flowers at its base. 'I love you.'

'Are you ready?' Wilson asked. 'It's time we should go.'

Kane looked at Margaret. 'Are you sure you want to do this?'

Staring at Ryan's headstone, she said, 'Honestly? I've no idea. But Ryan isn't here any more. The only thing left is his memory. And we can take that with us.'

Three days ago, sitting in Kane's living room with coffee and sympathies, Wilson had told Kane their plan. As long as Bernhard's associates were running free, they could never guarantee his safety, could not guarantee the safety of Margaret in her cell.

Kane had held his coffee mug between numb fingers and listened as Wilson said, 'Witness protection.'

Clark had specified, 'There'd be certain conditions. You'd be given a new name; we'll get you some start-up money; a new job. But you can't come back here. Not until it's over. You can have no contact with anyone.'

Kane had thought about it before asking, 'What about Margaret? I can't leave her. I'm all she has.'

Wilson and Clark had shared a look, a smile. 'It's highly unethical,' Wilson said, 'but we've already broken so many rules.'

'What are you saying?' he asked them.

'She's going with you,' Clark said.

'How will you get her out of prison?'

Wilson drank the last of his coffee and said, 'Leave that to us.'

Now, he reached into his back pocket and withdrew a photograph, unfolded it, stared at it: he and Ryan, arm in arm, on Ryan's seventeenth birthday. He placed the photograph beside the flowers and stood. It had been taken eight years ago when they were newly in love and felt that they had the whole world at their feet. And eight years ago, as they lay in bed together that night, they knew their love would last forever.

Kane put a hand to his chest as Margaret touched his back.

'I'm ready now,' she said.

Kane looked around, saw the police officer scuffing his shoe in the dirt, and recognised him as Officer Richards, the policeman who had watched over him that first night in his flat, a time that felt so long ago now.

Richards smiled at him, turned his back on them.

Wilson smirked. 'Richards is one of ours,' he said. 'I told you we were watching you before you came to London.'

Clark checked her watch. 'Look, if we're going to give you a new life, we need to do it now.' She waved her arm and Kane's guards stepped from shadows and trees.

'Ready?' Wilson asked.

Kane nodded.

And looking down at the photograph, at Ryan's smiling face, he began to remember.

—

Margaret had kept Ryan in the kitchen when Kane had come in through the front door carrying his birthday present, a five-foot by three-foot rectangle wrapped in silver paper.

When Ryan burst through the kitchen door and into Kane's arms, wearing a silly party hat, Kane laughed and said, 'I didn't realise it was your fifth birthday!'

'You love it,' Ryan said, and he forced Kane to wear one, too.

Kane gave him the present and said, 'When I saw it, I had to get it for you.'

'What is it?'

'Open it.'

They settled together on the plush sofa and Ryan tore at the paper. When he had exposed the present and turned it the right way up, he smiled wider than Kane could ever think possible.

'I love it!' Ryan said and threw his arms around Kane's neck. Eight years later, that canvas painting of Bette Davis still hung in their flat.

Ryan kissed him and Margaret backed her way in from the kitchen. She turned, grinned, and held up a cake with 'Happy 17th Birthday' iced onto it and seventeen candles glowing and flickering like a fence around its edges.

She began to sing. 'Happy birthday to you, happy birthday to you…'

Kane stood and pulled Ryan to his feet as he joined in with the song.

Ryan was grinning and singing and laughing.

And Margaret was singing and dancing and twirling.

And Kane put his arms around Ryan and pressed his forehead to his temple. 'Happy birthday,' he said.

And they kissed.

ಸಾ

Peter J Merrigan is the author of
THE CAMEL TRAIL
RIDER
LYNCH

And the forthcoming title
THE BATTLE FOR AILIGH

Find him online at
peterjmerrigan.co.uk

Printed in Poland
by Amazon Fulfillment
Poland Sp. z o.o., Wrocław